DARK ENEMY TAKEN

CHILDREN OF THE GODS BOOK 4

I. T. LUCAS

THE CHILDREN OF THE GODS

TRY THE SERIES ON

AUDIBLE

2 FREE audiobooks with your new Audible subscription!

CHAPTER 1: AMANDA

"*N*ice driving," Amanda said as Dalhu slammed on the brakes and took a sharp turn. The car swerved, skidding on the loose gravel, then finally coming to a full stop just inches away from a rusted metal gate.

After driving for hours through the dark forest, the Doomer had apparently reached his final destination. This private dirt road must've led to the mountain cabin he was planning to hide in.

Dear Fates, how could her life have taken such a sharp turn into the twilight zone in the span of just a few hours? In her craziest dreams, or rather worst nightmares, Amanda could not have foreseen being captured by a Doomer. No other female of their clan had ever fallen into the hands of their vicious enemy—the minions-of-all-that-is-evil—

the Brotherhood of the *Devout Order Of Mortdh* —Doomers.

But why had the vengeful Fates doomed her to be the first? What had she done to earn their wrath? What wrong could she have possibly committed to deserve such punishment?

Everything had been going so well.

Maybe too well…

Enjoying too much success or too much happiness without giving the Fates credit for the good fortune they bestowed was never wise.

Amanda had been basking in the success of her research. She'd finally been able to identify two excellent potential Dormants and even managed to convince Kian, her stubborn and skeptic brother, to allow the process of their activation to begin. Amanda had high hopes for both. Syssi, her adorable lab assistant, was an exceptional seer, and Michael, a student, was an excellent receiving telepath. And what's more, Kian had fallen head over heels for Syssi, just as Amanda had known he would, and he was attempting the girl's activation himself.

Am I a fabulous matchmaker or what?

But the Fates were capricious and must've been angered by her vanity. She should've thanked them for their help and should've given them credit for her success.

Please forgive me? I want my old life back.

Only this morning, she'd taken Syssi on a fun day of beauty salons and shopping, after which they'd met with Andrew, Syssi's wickedly attractive brother, for lunch.

She should've stayed with them; she should've gone home with Syssi.

But Amanda had wanted to do something nice for Syssi.

She sighed; *no good deed goes unpunished.*

She'd wanted to commission a duplicate of the pendant Syssi had given her. The lovely diamond-encrusted heart was Andrew's gift to Syssi for her sixteenth birthday. Amanda wanted to prevent any unpleasantries between Andrew and Syssi in case he discovered that his sister had given away his gift. So she'd said goodbye, leaving them behind in the restaurant, and headed out on her own to the jewelry store, back to Rodeo Drive.

It had happened there.

She had been kidnapped. By a Doomer. In broad daylight. From the Beverly Hills jewelry store.

How is that for drama?

Though, unfortunately, not of her own making —for a change.

Dear Fates, Syssi and Kian must be going out of their minds with worry.

Or maybe not.

They're most likely busy declaring their love for each other over that romantic dinner Kian promised Syssi, or maybe they're already back at Kian's penthouse—making love...

Not that Amanda wasn't ecstatic for them. After all, it had been her brilliant matchmaking that had brought Syssi and Kian together.

She couldn't help worrying, though. Their happily-ever-after was far from guaranteed. If Syssi didn't turn immortal, their fairy-tale love story would end in tragedy.

Because letting Syssi go would destroy Kian.

Unfortunately, he'd be forced to do it. As much as Amanda would've wished for a different solution, she had to accept that there was no other way.

Even if they made an exception for Syssi, allowing her to keep knowledge of their existence, the sad fact was that her human life span was a blink of an eye compared to Kian's near immortal one. Kian would have no choice but to send her away and erase her memory—of him and everything else to do with the existence of immortals.

Though, in truth, what purpose could it serve for Syssi to retain her memories? Memories that would remind her of the great love she'd found and lost?

None.

Erasing them would be a mercy. There was no reason for Syssi to suffer along with Kian. Pity that there was no way to erase an immortal's memory —it could have saved him the anguish.

Unless…

Perhaps it was possible their mother could do it for him. As the only surviving pure-blooded goddess, Annani had the power to manipulate immortal minds—just as immortals had the power to manipulate those of humans. Maybe she'd be able to help him.

Except, Kian would most likely refuse. Knowing her brother, Amanda suspected that he would welcome the torment. The poor guy would believe that he deserved the punishment.

Though, if he wanted to assign blame, he should pick her.

Kian would've never attempted Syssi's activation if not for Amanda's insistence. Initially, he'd refused. Not that she could fault his reasoning. To the contrary, while Amanda was willing to bend clan law and her sense of honor for the greater good, Kian held himself to higher standards.

The act of seducing a potential dormant female and injecting her with venom to facilitate the activation of her dormant genes was morally iffy. Especially since, out of necessity, the attempted activation had to be done without her consent— her memory of it erased. Not to mention that the probability of it working was extremely low.

Nonexistent—in Kian's opinion.

Eventually, though, Kian's attraction to Syssi had overpowered his good conscience and honorable intentions and he'd seduced the girl. But somewhere along the line he'd fallen in love with her and had told her the truth.

About everything.

Yeah, if Syssi didn't turn, Kian would blame himself for lacking the willpower to stay away from her.

Dear Fates, please, let Syssi turn...

And please, help me get away from this crazy Doomer... Crazy, but, sigh, so incredibly handsome...

As Dalhu bent over the padlock, working to open it and remove the chain that held the gate fastened to the fence, his muscular arms flexed and his T-shirt clung to his strong back. Amanda just couldn't help but admire what he was putting on display.

He must be at least six-seven or eight... Very appealing for a tall female like me...

Bad Amanda! Stop ogling the evil Doomer!

She averted her gaze when Dalhu returned and folded his huge frame inside. He drove the car a few feet past the gate, then stopped and got out to relock it behind them.

It was a little past midnight when he parked the car at the end of the long, private driveway, in front of the isolated mountain cabin.

Observing the so-called cabin, Amanda grimaced. Dalhu had obviously chosen the place based on how well hidden it was. Style, or even comfort, hadn't been factored in.

The place was dreadful. Calling it a cabin was a joke. She'd stayed at mountain cabins before, and this dingy shack didn't deserve the appellation. And what's worse, it was completely and utterly isolated. The last time she'd spotted signs of habitation, including power poles and power lines, had been over an hour ago. And it wasn't as if the electric cables were buried in the ground. At some point, the power lines had just veered away from the road and into the mountains, disappearing from view.

What had the Doomer been thinking? That she would gather wood and schlep water from a well?

Can you say delusional? Amanda humphed and crossed her arms over her chest.

Dalhu shot her an amused glance. "Come on, Professor, let's see what we got here."

She hated when he called her *Professor* in that mocking tone of his—as if she was delusional despite being well educated. "I asked you not to call me that…"

"Sorry, I just love saying it, *Professor*…"

Insufferable male…

He got out and walked up to the front porch—looking annoyingly cheerful. Evidently, the Doomer deemed this rundown shack to be just great. In his defense, though, she had no doubt this was a step up from what he'd been used to.

Whatever, she'd better take a good look around and check for anything that might give her some advantage—a way out. Trouble was, she had no idea what to look for.

Should've watched some adventure movies… about escape from captivity… Oh, well, should've and could've are not going to help me now.

Stepping out of the car, Amanda followed Dalhu—taking tiny, slow steps. It was dark. There was no artificial lighting coming out from the cabin, and the moon was obscured by heavy, dark clouds. Still, as an immortal, her night vision was excellent, and the little light filtering through the cover of clouds was enough. To her great relief, she saw that there would be no need for her to schlep wood or water to the cabin. Power was provided by a solar panel array that covered one side of the steep roof and a wind turbine that towered over the main building. There was another small structure a few feet away, probably storage, and what looked like a water well next to it. The contraption on top of the well must be an electrical pump. At least she hoped it was electrical... Amanda still remembered times when most people had to do with manual pumps—not that she'd ever done any pumping, that was what servants were for.

Oh, Fates, I miss Onidu.

Onidu, her loyal butler, who was always there for her, taking care of her and doing all of the boring housework tasks. Right now, if he were here, she would hug him and wouldn't let go—and it didn't matter at all that Onidu wasn't a real person, only a brilliant technological construct.

Fully aware that he had no real feelings, she loved him anyway. How could she not? Even though it was his programming that was responsible for all that he had done for her since she was little, like keep her company, take care of her, protect her...

Get a grip, Amanda! she commanded herself, fighting the tears that were stinging the back of her eyes. She had mere seconds to finish assessing her environment before Dalhu finished his breaking and entering and hauled her inside.

It seemed that, unfortunately, the cabin was self-sufficient and off the grid. The chances of anyone being able to follow her trail to this remote and isolated place were slim to none, and so were her opportunities to run or get help.

It took Dalhu no more than a few seconds to manipulate the lock and open the door. By the time she climbed the two steps leading up to the porch, he was already inside, flipping the light switch on.

The downstairs was only one room, with an ugly L-shaped kitchen and a narrow wooden staircase leading up to an open loft-style bedroom. Both were sparsely furnished with old, worn out furniture that was covered with a thick layer of dust and decorated with an appalling number of spider webs.

Ugh, so disgusting.

Standing by the entry, she clutched her twenty-thousand-dollar-plus purse close to her body, keeping it away from the grime, and glanced around in search of the bathroom. There was only one door in the whole place that looked like it could lead to another room, and it was upstairs in the loft bedroom.

She imagined the bathroom was just as dirty and disgusting as the rest of the place, but nature was calling, and crouching behind some bush in the middle of the night was not happening. "I'm going to pee and take a bath. In the meantime, you'd better start cleaning. The place is filthy." Amanda took the stairs up to the loft and strode into the bathroom.

She made sure to lock the door behind her.

Not that she had any illusions that it could keep Dalhu out if he decided he wanted in. But she hoped he would have the decency to get a clue and stay out. Until now, the Doomer had proven to be surprisingly courteous and civil—*for a kidnapper, that is, and a Doomer*. She was expecting him to behave like a gentleman, which probably meant that Dalhu wasn't the only one who was delusional here.

"Doomer" and "gentleman" just didn't belong in the same sentence.

"Pampered brat...," she heard him mumble under his breath as she wiped the dusty toilet seat with tissue paper. Thank heavens she'd found some that had been leftover by the previous occupant because she hadn't thought to bring it up from the car.

"I heard that!" she said, flushing it down.

The gall of the man, calling her a pampered brat. Not that he was wrong, necessarily—she was pampered... and a brat... but as her kidnapper, he had no right to expect her to be considerate.

Amanda slid a disgusted glance over the dirty tub and sighed. She would have to clean the thing herself. But how? She had never cleaned anything before.

Maybe filling it with water and then draining it would do the trick.

The rusty, old faucet made an ominous screeching sound when she forced it to turn, and waiting to see what would come out of it, Amanda held her breath. As she'd expected, the water was brown with rust from the old pipes and whatever other nasties. But when after a few seconds it ran clean, Amanda breathed out.

She flicked the toilet lid closed and sat down. Waiting for the tub to fill, she let her head drop back.

Oh, dear Fates, what am I going to do?

With her gone, there would be no one to continue her research.

All her hard work, the long years she'd spent studying and working toward earning her PhD. in neuroscience and then carving out a position for herself at the university—gone—because of one fateful coincidence. Why were the Fates so cruel to her? Just as she had finally found what she'd been searching for, they had taken it away from her.

The university would probably replace her with another professor who would continue her lab's formal research. But there would be no one to conduct her unofficial experiments on mortals with paranormal abilities; no one to search for possible dormant carriers of her people's immortal genes. Amanda had been so close to finding a solution to her clan members' lonely existence. The matriarch of their clan, Annani, was the only known surviving full-blooded goddess, but that didn't mean that some of the immortal female descendants of other goddesses hadn't survived the cataclysm.

As long as Amanda was Dalhu's captive, she wouldn't know if Syssi and Michael did indeed descend from other goddesses. But if they'd transitioned, at least two members of her clan would gain lifelong partners.

Amanda sighed. What if she'd been wrong?

Perhaps she'd been deluding herself.

Syssi most likely wasn't a Dormant, and neither was Michael. What if Amanda had given Kian false hope, condemning both her brother and Syssi to terrible heartache? Or worse?

Because if Syssi didn't turn, Kian would be devastated.

He would blame Amanda.

And he'd be right.

Long-term relationships between mortals and immortals weren't possible, not only due to the disparity in life spans, but also because of the risk of exposure. No one in the mortal world was allowed to know about the existence of immortals, no exceptions. It was an existential necessity.

Syssi, thank the merciful Fates, would be spared the pain because she wouldn't remember falling in love with Kian. But losing Syssi would destroy Kian.

At best, Kian and Syssi could have a couple of months together. Any longer and Syssi might suffer irreversible brain damage from having too many memories suppressed. And even if she were to escape neurological damage, she might be driven insane by the large chunk of time missing from her life and the inevitable surfacing of bits and pieces of confusing memories.

No!

This time, Amanda wasn't wrong. She could feel it in her gut. Syssi would turn, and so would Michael. And if she'd managed to find two potential Dormants just by conducting a few small-scale experiments in her university lab, then there must be many more out there.

At last she could ensure a better future for her clan and put an end to the lonely existence they had been forced to endure for centuries.

That's right; she would earn the respect of her family, transcending the image of a spoiled princess. Amanda's mood improved considerably. There was just one small obstacle she still had to overcome.

She had to escape.

CHAPTER 2: DALHU

"*I* heard that!" Amanda called while flushing the toilet.

"Good!" he answered.

As he climbed up the rickety stairs with a load of shopping bags in each hand, Dalhu's full bladder demanded immediate attention. He dropped the bags on the dusty bed cover and waited for Amanda to be done.

But then, a squeak of an old faucet followed by the sound of water hitting the bottom of a tub made him realize that the selfish woman had started the water for a bath without giving a second thought to the fact that he might need to use the bathroom as well.

No big deal, he could take care of business outside.

Once that most pressing need was satisfied, Dalhu finished unloading the supplies he'd pilfered from the general store—well, it wasn't really pilfering since he'd left money on the counter to cover what he'd taken. After dropping the last load on the kitchen floor, he went back to the Honda and drove it off the driveway. Hiding it in the thicket, he made sure it was well covered with dense greenery—in case someone thought to do an aerial search for the missing car. The keys went under the floorboards of the porch, safely hidden and out of Amanda's reach.

Back in the cabin, Dalhu appraised the thick layer of dust covering every exposed surface and the spider webs hanging from ceiling corners and between furniture legs. The place was indeed filthy, but it was so small that he would have no problem cleaning all of it while the spoiled princess soaked in the tub. And hopefully, by the time he was done, he would manage to work up a little sweat…

Imagining Amanda's lustful response to his half-naked, glistening body, he felt a surge of arousal. Since she'd admitted to fantasizing about him like that, he planned to exploit her weakness.

He was one lucky SOB. So lucky that he still had a hard time believing it.

For a change, the Fates had smiled kindly upon him, bringing him to the right place at the right time to snatch the first immortal female he'd ever encountered. And not just any immortal female, but the beautiful professor he'd been lusting after since the first time he'd seen her picture—the one in the autographed magazine article his men had found in the clan programmer's house.

The programmer whose assassination Dalhu had ordered.

But she didn't have to know this, did she? Not yet anyway. First, he was going to seduce her, then he was going to win her heart, and only after he was sure she was his would he come clean.

Damn. Maybe he should just keep it from her forever. Who knew how close Amanda had been to that programmer. After all, she'd signed that picture for the guy with a personal dedication. And even if they hadn't been close, family was still family, and she might not be able to get over that hurdle.

But he knew in his gut that keeping a secret like that would fester like a human's malignant wound.

His best bet was to seduce her and get her addicted to him. He'd heard rumors that the venom was addictive. True, the rumors had only talked about mortal females, but it made sense that the same would hold true for immortal ones. After all, if the venom was indeed addictive, the original purpose must've been to get immortal females bound to their mates.

He would prefer not to rely on such an underhanded method, but it could become necessary in case he failed for some reason to win Amanda's heart. She would get hooked on him no matter what. And anyway, it wasn't as if he could do anything to prevent it. With a wicked smile tugging at the corner of his mouth, Dalhu took off his shirt and went to work.

"Game on, Professor."

The first thing on his agenda was the dusty mattress. Dalhu climbed the stairs up to the loft and eyed the shopping bags he'd dumped on the bed.

Well, that hadn't been smart.

He took them down to the floor, then removed the bedding and dropped it over the railing down to the ground floor. Carefully, he hefted the mattress and lifted it over his head. It wasn't heavy, but maneuvering it down the narrow stairs and out the front door without banging into the walls forced him to go slower than he would've liked.

He left the mattress braced against the porch railing and jogged to the kitchen to grab a broom.

As he pounded the mattress, he had to shield his nose and mouth with his other hand against the clouds of dust billowing out of it. The whole porch rattled and shook as he kept beating at the thing. Hopefully, the railing was sturdy enough to absorb the force of his strikes. When he was satisfied that no amount of additional pounding would cause the thing to release more dust, he hefted the mattress back up to the loft. But as he dropped it over the box spring, producing a new cloud, Dalhu realized that he should've given the box the same treatment as the mattress. No time, though. There was still a lot to clean, and he wanted to be done before Amanda finished her bath.

With a quick jog down the stairs, he got to the pile of bedding he'd dropped and scooped it up from the floor. He headed toward what he thought was a utility room, but there was no washer in the broom closet next to the kitchen that he'd mistaken for one. If there was a washer in the cabin at all, it must've been stashed in the bathroom upstairs. He could think of no other place where it could've been hidden.

Maybe it was in the shack outside? He'd check later, but, for now, stuffing it in the broom closet would do. First, though, he had to take out the vacuum cleaner to make room for the bundle.

He was about to attack the floor with the ancient machine when it crossed his mind that the sofa was probably in no better shape than the mattress.

It took two more trips out to the porch and some more pounding with the broom to liberate the heavy layer of dust from the sofa cushions.

Back to the floors.

Though not much to look at, the simple vacuum cleaner was doing a decent job—for a little while. Dalhu stopped when the loud engine changed its tune from a drone to a whine, and a slight burning scent reached his nose.

Good that he had or the thing would've gone up in smoke. After examining the various components, he found a canister that needed emptying.

Live and learn.

Cleaned, the thing worked perfectly again. Once the floors looked passable, Dalhu wiped the rest of the surfaces with a couple of wet rags, then disposed of them the same way he did the bedding —into the broom closet.

Later, he planned to put everything in the washer. If there was one. If not, he was going to throw the stuff in the trash. As it was, he'd already exceeded his lifelong quota of domestic activity. Washing by hand was not going to happen unless the professor volunteered to do it...

Yeah... hell has a better chance of freezing over...

The things he was willing to do for a woman. At his home base, Dalhu wouldn't have been caught dead holding a broom. A warrior carried a rifle or a sword—only servants and trainees carried cleaning implements and did the kinds of jobs he had done tonight.

Dalhu rubbed his neck, his hand coming away oily with sweat. He smirked, wiping his palm on his dirty jeans.

Mission accomplished.

It was time to present himself to the bathing princess. Except, now that he was done, an insidious doubt drifted through his mind, and his plan suddenly seemed foolish. What if she screamed at him to get out? Or looked at him with disgust in her beautiful blue eyes?

After all, he'd kidnapped her, drugged her, and had cuffed her to a bed. It was a wonder Amanda was talking to him at all, or looking at him with anything other than fear, or even worse —loathing.

Dalhu sighed. It was what it was. He would do his best with the cards fate had dealt him—the good and the bad, and there was no place for doubts or second thoughts if he wanted to win the most important game of his life.

Winners didn't cower before a challenge.

They embraced it.

Amanda was going to be his.

Climbing the wooden stairs, he made sure to stomp his feet and make his approach as loud as possible. What little sense of propriety he possessed demanded that he at least let Amanda know he was coming and give the female a chance to cover herself before he barged in on her.

With his hand on the bathroom door's handle, Dalhu hesitated for a fraction of a moment before plastering a confident though totally fake grin on his face and forcing his way in. "Hello, princess," he said, the words he'd prepared on his way up.

It was good that he'd spoken as soon as he had, because the sight of Amanda's perfect body laid out in the bathtub in all its naked glory had rendered him speechless.

And the way she was looking at him, basking in the knowledge of the effect she had on him…

There was no shame in her eyes, no attempt to cover her perfect breasts with her hands. If anything, the woman seemed to feed off his stunned stupor.

"Dalhu, darling, as soon as you're done drooling, could you please bring me the toiletries and a towel? Don't forget the conditioner…"

He barely heard the words coming out of that gorgeous mouth.

What did she say? Soap and towel?

Damn, Dalhu swallowed, his brain short-circuiting from all the visual stimuli. Fully clothed, Amanda was stunning; naked, she was like a stroke of lightning—awe-inspiring and deadly. Because if he were mortal, his heart would have surely stopped.

Dalhu wiped a shaky hand over his mouth. Dimly aware that he had a plan coming up here and forcing his way into the bathroom, he struggled to remember what it was, but with most of his neurons misfiring it was hard to concentrate.

There was something that was supposed to turn her on…

Yeah… and I'm doing such a great job of it… as if gawking and drooling is going to do it for her…

Fuck! What a splendid personification of masculinity he was displaying…

Pull yourself together, you idiot!

Showing weakness wouldn't do with a woman like her…

Not a woman—a fucking goddess…

He'd better pull his shit together and project

24

strength and confidence before he lost her respect...

If he'd ever had it to begin with.

At first, when he'd grabbed her in that jewelry store, she'd been terrified of him. But then, after he'd bitten her, overloading her system with his venom, she'd begged him to fuck her like a common slut. But that was the venom's doing; she'd been high on its aphrodisiac properties. He had no doubt that she would've never acted like that when sober. And that's why, as hard as it had been, he'd refused her pleas. In his mind, to oblige her would've been akin to rape.

Trouble was, the way she'd cussed at him for refusing her, Dalhu doubted his restraint had been appreciated. He wondered whether by treating her honorably he'd gained her respect or had lost it altogether.

Perhaps he'd been stupid for wanting her sober consent, but this was not about an easy lay. This woman was his future, and he'd be damned if he'd screw things up by taking advantage of her in a compromised state.

Hopefully, once she sobered up and remembered, she'd appreciate his gallantry.

Except, one could never know with women...

Still, even if she'd found his behavior gallant, it

didn't mean she thought highly of him. Most likely, Amanda considered him beneath her.

Not nearly good enough.

And he wasn't—not by a long shot.

He was aware that Amanda found him attractive, but that was about it—his only redeeming quality. She was a professor while he was an uneducated mercenary. She was rich, and he wasn't. Not to mention the little issue of him kidnapping her and holding her prisoner with no intention of ever letting her go…

Or being her family's sworn enemy…

"The toiletries, Dalhu? And the towel?" she repeated, her eyes twinkling with amusement. The woman knew she had him by the balls… and not just figuratively…

"Coming right up, princess." Dalhu forced a smile before tearing his eyes away.

Damn. Now he was sweating worse than he had from the physical work he'd done before. Thank Mortdh, he'd been already covered in sweat when he'd come in… maybe she wouldn't notice it had gotten worse… because of her…

The woman had him wrapped around her little finger and doing her bidding as if she was the one calling the shots.

She was, though, wasn't she?

He would do anything to please her.

Except, Amanda might think she had gained the upper hand, but in the grand scheme of things, her victory was an illusion. It played right into his plan. Dalhu was fully committed to doing whatever was necessary to win her over, and to that end —to please her—he was willing to go places and do things he'd never endeavored before.

In the end, she would be his.

There was no way he was losing this most important campaign.

He took his time collecting Amanda's bathing paraphernalia—which was everything besides the soap, razor, and toothbrush that were his—the minute or two spent helping him get over the initial shock of seeing her naked. When he was done, Dalhu was ready to face her again.

Like a man…

"Thank you," she said when he came back with an armful of stuff he had no idea what she was going to do with. But what did he know? Perhaps all females required five different hair products and nine kinds of lotions.

"My pleasure." Leaning against the counter, he crossed his arms over his chest, purposefully. His bulging biceps producing the response he was hoping for. Amanda's appreciative glance had lingered before she shifted her gaze back to his face.

"Well, hand me the stuff and get out. The peep show is over."

"Which *staff* are you referring to?" Dalhu arched a brow.

Look at me, being all clever with the wordplay and all...

"Funny, aren't you?" Amanda feigned nonchalance, but couldn't help shooting a quick glance at the other bulging part of his body. "Just the soap, shampoo, and conditioner," she said a little throatily.

"You sure that's all you need, sweetheart?"

"Need and want in one hand, shit in the other—see what you get the most of..." She pinned him with her blue stare. "Get out, Dalhu, I mean it."

"Yes, ma'am." He saluted and pushed off the counter. "Don't take too long, though, I'm of a mind to get in there with you... As you can see, I'm dirty." He looked down his pecs, flexing, "Absolutely filthy." He winked and walked out.

Closing the door behind him was a no go because the handle was broken and the thing wouldn't stay closed, but he did the best he could, leaving it only slightly ajar.

He exhaled the breath he was holding and

picked up his shirt from the floor, using it to wipe the sweat off his face and his chest. Well, that hadn't turned out a complete fiasco. When he'd finally been able to think with something other than his dick, he'd noticed the way Amanda had been struggling with her own lust.

Things were not going as smoothly as he'd anticipated, but then nothing ever did. All good things were worth waiting for, and though he didn't think he'd be waiting much longer, if need be, he would.

After all, time was on his side. The way he'd carefully covered their trail, no one was going to come to Amanda's rescue anytime soon.

CHAPTER 3: AMANDA

*A*s she heard Dalhu exhale a relieved breath from behind the bathroom door, Amanda smirked with satisfaction.

Dalhu's surprised expression when he'd burst into the bathroom had been priceless. Seeing her in all her nude glory with her body boldly displayed in the bath's clear water—not gasping or trying to cover herself as most women would—the guy had been rendered speechless.

But then she was nothing like what he was used to.

Not even close.

Amanda was the daughter of a goddess, for fate's sake.

He hadn't been the only one affected, though. As he'd devoured her with his hungry eyes, her body had responded, her nipples growing taut under his hooded gaze.

Ogling her, he'd wiped the drool off his mouth with the back of his dirty hand, looking just as awestruck as one of her students. But that was where the resemblance ended.

Dalhu was a magnificent specimen of manhood, and in comparison, all her former partners looked like mere boys. Shirtless and sweaty, he'd looked just as amazing as she'd imagined he would.

He was big; not even Yamanu was that tall, and Dalhu was more powerfully built. Nevertheless, his well-defined muscles were perfectly proportioned for his size with no excess bulk; he looked strong, but not pumped like someone who spent endless hours lifting weights at a gym.

Following the light smattering of dark hair trailing down the center of his chest to where it disappeared below the belt line of his jeans, she hadn't been surprised to find that he was well proportioned everywhere. And as he kept staring at her, mesmerized, his jeans growing too tight to contain him, she'd held her breath in anticipation of her first glimpse of that magnificent length.

Oh, boy, am I in a shitload of trouble.

There was just no way she could resist all that

yummy maleness. Amanda knew she was going to succumb to temptation.

She always had.

Except, this time, she would be stooping lower than ever. Because she could think of nothing that would scream SLUT louder than her going willingly into the arms of her clan's mortal enemy...

Shit, damn, damn, shit... she cursed silently.

It had taken sheer willpower to kick him out. She so hadn't wanted to...

But she would've never been able to look at herself in the mirror if she'd succumbed to the impulse and had dragged him down into that bathtub to have her wicked way with him.

Hopefully, he'd been too busy hiding his own reaction to have noticed hers.

What was it about him that affected her so? Yes, he was incredibly handsome, and she was a lustful hedonist... but, come on, she had been a hair away from jumping the guy...

Was she one of those women that got turned on by bad boys?

Yep, evidently I am.

How shameful...

Her hand sneaked down to the juncture of her thighs, and she let her finger slide over the slick wetness that had nothing to do with the water she was soaking in. But after a quick glance at the door that wouldn't close, she gritted her teeth and pulled her fingers away from the seat of her pleasure.

She couldn't let Dalhu know how he affected her if she hoped to have a chance of keeping him off her.

And herself off him…

Damn!

She had to keep telling herself over and over again, repeating it like a mantra until it sunk in, that there was nothing that would scream SLUT louder than her going willingly into the arms of a Doomer.

Oh Fates, I'm such a slut…

But wait… this was it…the solution to her predicament…

If there was one thing that was sure to shatter Dalhu's romantic illusions, it was to find out that the woman he wanted for his mate had been with a shitload of others before him.

She was well acquainted with the Doomers' opinions about women and their place in society. Someone like her probably would get stoned to death in the parts of the world they controlled. And though Dalhu seemed smarter and better informed than the average Doomer, he no doubt believed in the same old double standard. It was perfectly okay for him to fuck a different woman every night because his body demanded it. But it was not okay for her.

She was supposed to suffer the pain like a good little girl because decent women were not supposed to want or enjoy sex...

Well, she not only wanted it and enjoyed it, but needed it to survive, just like any other near-immortal male or female.

But try explaining it to a Doomer...

Stupid. Blind. Deaf.

Members of the brotherhood of the "Devout Order Of Mortdh" were brainwashed to hate women and believed them to be inferior and unworthy. It was sad, really, how easy it was for Navuh and his propaganda to affect not only his followers, and not only the male population of the regions under his control, but also the women living there. They succumbed to the same beliefs, accepting that they were inferior, that being abused was their due, and that that was what their god wanted for them.

The poor things didn't know any better.

If a girl heard all throughout her life that she was worthless, and her education was limited to basic literacy at best, she was going to believe it, buying into the label she'd been given and perceiving herself that way.

Thinking back to her own youth in Scotland, and even later in their new home in America, the situation for women had been only slightly better. Though they were not as badly mistreated as their counterparts in Navuh's region, the prevailing attitude, sadly, had been similar up until recent times. Women had been considered not as smart and not as capable as men, but at least their mothering and homemaking skills had been appreciated. For most of her life, women had accepted these beliefs as immutable truths, treating the few that had tried to rise above them as bad mothers, misguided individuals, and an undesirable influence on their daughters.

Thank heavens this was changing. There was still discrimination in the workforce, with men getting better pay and faster promotions, but at least the West was on the right track.

Oh, well, her mother and the rest of their clan did what they could. But where Navuh had his clutches deeply in the hearts of mortals there was nothing to be done.

They were lost souls.

As was Dalhu.

The guy struggled against what he was, though,

she had to hand him that. But could he break free after the centuries of brainwashing he'd suffered?

As a scientist, Amanda knew there was no hope for him. But as a person, as a woman… well… hope was for children and fools—as Kian was fond of saying.

She wasn't a child… so that left being a fool…

Still, hopeful or not, how was she going to get the guy disillusioned with her without getting him so enraged that he would chop her head off?

Dalhu was unstable, going from rage to affection in a heartbeat, and she was afraid of what he'd do if she told him the truth about whom he was planning to spend his life with.

Perhaps the smart thing to do was to bide her time and wait to be rescued.

But how would anyone even know where to look for her?

Damn. What to do… what to do…

Wait… but what if she let Dalhu have her…

Just so he wouldn't kill her… of course…

That wouldn't count as her going to him willingly, would it?

And if she didn't suffer horribly in the process… well…

Now that she'd come up with a semi-moral excuse for sleeping with the enemy—only if it became necessary of course—her mood improved, and she hurried to finish soaping, shampooing, and conditioning before Dalhu got tired of waiting and decided to jump in the tub with her.

Having the option didn't mean she should court that particular outcome, did it?

She finished drying off with the cheap, coarse towel and wrapped it around her body with a grimace. It was way too short, barely covering her butt.

Clutching the shitty towel so it would cover at least her nipples on top and the juncture of her thighs on the bottom, she walked out of the bathroom.

"Not a word, Dalhu. Not a fucking word…" she hissed at his ogling smirk, the cuss word feeling foreign and vulgar on her lips.

He arched a brow but said nothing. Grabbing a pair of gray sweats, he tore off the price tags and ducked into the bathroom she'd just vacated.

There was another set of sweats folded on top of the bed… pink… and plain cotton panties… also pink…

Her lips twisted in distaste. "Oh, goody, that must be for me."

With a quick glance behind her, she made sure the bathroom door was closed, or as well as it could be, before dropping the towel. With a sigh, she reluctantly shimmied into the cheap panties and then pulled on the shapeless, polyester-blend sweats.

Her bare skin had never before touched anything as disgusting, and a glance at the mirror hanging over the bathroom door proved that she'd never before worn anything as ugly as this either.

She looked positively… well… blah.

The good news was that no one she knew was going to see her in this humiliating getup. Unfortunately, though, she was pretty sure that it didn't make her look ugly enough for Dalhu to lose interest either.

The bad news was that she had no idea how she was going to sleep with the horrible synthetic fabric irritating her skin. And sleeping naked was not an option—even if she made Dalhu sleep on the couch downstairs.

Sifting through the bags, she found the bedding she'd had him bring from the store. One scratchy sheet went over the naked mattress, then pillowcases over the two pillows, and another sheet under the comforter that, surprise, surprise, was also made from polyester…

Had there been nothing else in that store? Or

had Dalhu chosen the worst stuff to torture her with…

Well, payback is a bitch.

Grabbing a pillow and a woven blanket, she hurried down the stairs and dropped them on the couch. The thing was too short for Dalhu's huge body, and hopefully, it was lumpy as well…

"Sleep tight… hope you get lots of bedbug bites…" she singsonged as she walked over to the kitchen.

The food supplies Dalhu had stolen from the store were on the floor, still in their paper bags, and as she began taking the stuff out and arranging it on the counter, her spirits sunk even further. Apparently, Dalhu's idea of nutrition was mostly canned meat, canned beans, a few cans of vegetables, sliced white bread, and peanut butter.

The only thing to brighten her mood was a can of ground coffee, but only momentarily—there was no coffeemaker.

Putting together a peanut butter sandwich was something even she could do, but making coffee without the benefit of a coffeemaker was above the level of her meager culinary skills.

A quick search through the cabinets yielded nothing more exciting than some pots and pans, but thank heavens, she found a can opener.

Scooping some of the coffee into a pot, Amanda filled it with water and turned on the electric stove. Trouble was, she had no idea what the ratio should be, or if it was even possible to make stovetop coffee.

Hopefully, it would be drinkable...

She was desperate for it.

As she arranged the rest of the supplies in the cabinets, the aroma wafting from the cooking coffee smelled delicious, and once it looked like it was done, she poured it into two cups and began making peanut butter sandwiches for Dalhu and herself.

CHAPTER 4: DALHU

*D*alhu glanced at the ridiculously short sweats he'd pulled on after showering. The sleeves reached a little below his elbows, and the shirt's bottom barely covered his bellybutton. He'd pulled and tied the waistband string as tight as it would go, but it was still too wide and the pants kept sliding down. The fucking double X must've been about the girth, not the length.

And it wasn't as if Dalhu was worried about flashing a pair of boxer shorts. He wasn't wearing any. He'd forgotten to include them in his supply procurement…

For a moment, he considered changing into one of the fancy designer jeans that he'd purchased at that Rodeo Drive boutique. The faggot salesman had insisted that they made Dalhu's ass look *fabulous*…

Fortunately, for the bastard, he'd been so helpful and pleasant before the *ass* remark that Dalhu had decided to let him live…

Had it been only this morning?

So much had happened since that he felt as if it had happened days ago.

How much had he paid for those jeans? A thousand? More?

At least he'd paid with a credit card and not cash. On the run, the card was useless and he was low on cash. He kept the card, though, just in case. Hopefully, the Brotherhood's bureaucrats wouldn't cancel it anytime soon.

The designer clothes he'd spent so much money on wouldn't be used for their original purpose, though, and the custom suit he'd ordered would remain unclaimed.

The only reason he'd needed those obscenely expensive clothes in the first place was to go hunting for the males of Amanda's clan in the lucrative nightclubs they frequented.

But he'd left that part of his life behind.

Hopefully, it wouldn't come chasing after him.

The reinforcements Dalhu had asked for were due to arrive any day now. Navuh was sending a large contingent this time, and he had no doubt someone higher up in the organization would be leading them. Dalhu had been a commander of a small unit. There was no way he would've been left to head the operation, regardless of the fact that discovering Annani's clan's elusive trail had been his achievement.

Whatever, it was of no consequence. He had abandoned the Brotherhood and its questionable crusade for good.

Heading for the staircase, he paused and looked at the two top windows flanking the fireplace. The exposed glass made him uneasy.

All the other windows had shutters, which he'd closed, but those two at the top had none. If there had been a tall ladder he could've used, he would've taped or nailed bed sheets over the glass, but as he'd searched the cabin and the attached woodshed, the only ladder he'd found was too short.

Those windows were a dead giveaway that someone was inside the cabin, and even though it was unlikely that anyone would be looking for Amanda out here in the mountains, Dalhu hated taking even that slight chance.

He would have to insist on as little lighting as possible.

With a curse, he jogged down the stairs, his scowl deepening as he took in the pillow and blanket the princess had prepared for him on the couch. Not for a moment did he entertain the notion that she'd intended to sleep there herself. But if she thought he would be a gentleman and cram himself into the thing, she had another think coming.

Spoiled brat...

A beautiful, sexy, spoiled brat...

Standing barefoot at the counter, Amanda was a vision—looking amazing even in the plain pink sweats he'd gotten her. The pants waistband, which was clearly too wide for her narrow waist, was rolled over a couple of times, and the loose pants hung low on her hips, allowing him a glimpse of the curve of her creamy white ass each time she bent.

And she'd made coffee and sandwiches...

Maybe there was hope for her after all.

"You are beautiful," Dalhu breathed as he walked up to stand behind her and nuzzled her long, smooth neck.

Surprised, she shivered before ducking sideways. "Cut it out, Dalhu," she bit out. "Sit down and drink your coffee. I hope you like it black and bitter because you didn't get any sugar or creamer."

"That's so sweet of you, taking care of me like that," he said as he sat down and picked up the coffee mug.

"Don't get used to that."

As Dalhu took a sip, he barely made it to the sink in time to spit the thing out. "Are you trying to poison me, woman? What the hell did you do?" He rushed back to the table, grabbing a peanut butter sandwich and taking a quick bite to get rid of the gritty taste.

"There is no coffeemaker, okay? What did you expect?" The hurt expression on Amanda's face made it obvious that she didn't ruin the coffee just to spite him. Grabbing the pot by the handle, she dumped its contents in the sink, then braced her hands on the rim and dropped her head. Her delicate shoulders began trembling.

Was she crying? Did he make her cry?

Way to go, asshole...

"Don't worry about it. I'll make a new one." He got behind her and tried to turn her around.

A sob escaped her throat as she shrugged his hands off her shoulders. "Everything you got from that store is disgusting; the towels, the bedding, the clothes... everything... even the food. The bread tastes like cardboard, and everything else is canned yuck. And now I can't even have a decent cup of coffee. It's just too much... I can't take it anymore..." She began sobbing in earnest.

Dalhu felt helpless. What the hell was he supposed to do now?

"Please don't cry. If you make me a list, I'll go and get you whatever you need. I'm sorry that there was nothing better at that general store... Oh, hell..." Forcing her to turn, he wrapped his arms around her, crushing her to him—her cheek to his pec.

She struggled, but he held her tightly against him, rubbing his palm over her heaving back until she gave up and sagged in his arms. Crying and sobbing into his sweatshirt for what seemed like forever, Amanda was killing him.

And although he was well aware that the coffee was just the last straw that had broken this strong, amazing woman, the guilt of failing to provide for her, like he'd promised her he would, was eating him alive.

As the sobbing subsided, he reached for a paper towel, and still holding her with one arm, handed her the thing.

"Thank you." Amanda hiccupped and blew her nose into the towel. Pushing away from him, she threw it into the sink and wiped her face with her sleeve before glancing up at him. "I must be a mess. Red nose and blotchy eyes…"

"You're beautiful. Always. In any shape or form." He dipped his knees to look into the blue pools of her eyes, wanting to kiss her so bad it hurt.

She smiled a little. "You're just saying it to make me feel better…"

"No, I mean it. Come, sit down, relax, and I'll make you a good cup of coffee to cheer you up." He led her to the dining table and pulled out a chair for her.

"Good luck. There is no cream or sugar. So even if you manage to brew a decent coffee, I wouldn't like it."

"Oh, but you've missed something when you put the cans away. We have some evaporated milk —it's both sweet and creamy."

CHAPTER 5: AMANDA

The coffee Dalhu made turned out to be pretty good. And as hungry and thirsty as Amanda was, even the peanut butter sandwich was okay… well, edible… barely…

"Feeling better?" Dalhu peered at her from across the table.

"Much. Though I still hold you to your promise to get me everything I need."

"To the best of my ability. Though don't expect me to drive all the way to Rodeo Drive to buy you clothes. I know you're used to luxury, and at some point, hopefully soon, I'll be able to provide you with whatever you want. But for now, you'll have to lower your standards a little."

Amanda waved a dismissive hand. "At this

point, I'll consider decent food and stuff not made from polyester a luxury."

"Tomorrow, I'll take care of it. I promise."

"Good."

In the silence that followed, Dalhu obliterated the rest of the sandwiches while Amanda sipped on her second cup of coffee, observing him from under her lashes. He wasn't the most graceful of eaters, stuffing his mouth with huge bites, half a sandwich at a time, and crumbs littered the table all around him. Still, it didn't bother her as it should have.

Usually, poor eating manners would immediately disqualify a guy from having a chance with her, but Dalhu wasn't just any other guy. For some reason, she thought he looked manly eating like a hungry beast, and instead of turning her off, his bad table manners were turning her on.

Damn, she was evidently so horny that anything and everything was a turn-on. She'd better get away from this hunk of a male before her resolve faltered and she jumped his bones.

The intensity with which she craved Dalhu wouldn't have been surprising if she had gone without sex for several days, but after only one? The night before the fateful lunch that had led to her abduction, she had been with two different guys in a row. It should've kept her sated at least for a couple of days.

Yeah, but they weren't Dalhu. An immortal male with an amazing physique, and fangs... Damn, the memory of that bite... it had been so erotic... *Shit, think of something else, quick before he scents my arousal... Famine, war...*

Amanda breathed out as the sad images did their job. "Well, I'm beat. I'm going up to bed. Good night, Dalhu." She pushed away from the table.

"You really expect me to sleep on that sofa?" Dalhu got up and took the dirty dishes to the sink.

"Yep." She headed for the stairs.

"Wait..." He followed behind her. "What if I promise to stay on my side of the bed like a good little boy? To make me sleep on that couch is a cruel and unusual punishment."

The big, bad Dalhu was eyeing her hopefully, but she had no intention of sleeping with the guy. Because one thing was sure, as horny as she was, if he got in that bed with her, she had no doubt they'd end up doing way more than sleeping.

"As I see it, you deserve a cruel and unusual punishment for kidnapping me and dragging me out here, and then torturing me with polyester."

Dalhu heaved a defeated sigh and hung his head

for a moment, but then lifted it a little to look at her with a naughty smirk. "Okay, but I want a kiss. Just one kiss and I promise not to take it any further. A little reward for my gentlemanly sacrifice."

Oh, hell, one kiss. He was asking for just one kiss. Amanda wanted so much more than that...

Except, even though Dalhu had promised not to take it any further, Amanda was afraid a team of horses wouldn't be able to hold *her* back...

Oh, what the hell...

"Okay," she breathed and closed her eyes, tilting her head up.

His lips were incredibly soft and gentle as he brushed them against hers. Cupping her cheek with a tender palm, he kissed her, just a light stroke of mouth on mouth with hardly any pressure behind the contact. So sweet. Innocent.

A lover's kiss.

But it was enough to send an overwhelmingly erotic shudder through her, and she fought the urge to pull him down and kiss him the way a man like him should be kissed... Hard.

They both groaned, but it was Dalhu who pulled away first.

"For the love of Mortdh..." he hissed, turning around in a futile attempt to hide the tent that had sprouted in his sweatpants. "Please, just go. I want you so much, it hurts…"

Her eyes glued to the enormous erection he was trying to hide, Amanda was dimly aware that Dalhu was saying something.

Oh, dear Fates… that would feel so incredible inside me…

And the prospect of another bite…

As a flood of moisture pooled in her panties, Amanda closed her eyes. And as she relived that bite in her mind, the coiling sensation inside her got tighter and tighter, threatening to culminate in a climax.

Gritting her teeth, she fisted her hands and pushed the image away.

What the hell?

Fates knew that there had been plenty of times when she'd been horny, and a few days without sex would usually send her climbing up the walls—or the first attractive male she managed to snag—but she'd never orgasmed just from imagining it…

When Dalhu turned to her, he was all predator, his nostrils flaring with the scent of her arousal.

Oh, no…

No, no, no.

This was so bad…

They were both lost.

With Dalhu's fangs punching over his bottom lip and his eyes glowing, there was very little of the man left—he was mostly beast now—a beast who smelled a female in heat…

She had to stop him… and there was only one way she knew how…

"You're not the only one in pain. Do you know anything about immortal females?" She threw out a hand to stop him.

"I know everything I need to know…" he hissed through his fangs, his whole body somehow getting even bigger and scarier.

"Do you know that we are exactly like the males in our need for sex?"

"Good, then there is no reason for you to refuse me…" He smiled, though with his fangs out the smile wasn't exactly reassuring.

Here it goes…

Amanda swallowed audibly. It was now or never because she was already out of time. "I'm over two hundred years old, and since reaching the age of majority, which is seventeen among my people, I've been with a different guy almost every night…" she blurted in a hurry.

Dalhu looked as if someone had dumped a bucket of ice on his head. His fangs retracted and the tent in his pants deflated.

Which was good...

But the murderous look in his eyes was not... not good at all...

Whipping around, Amanda sprinted up the stairs—even though she had no clue where the hell she was going to hide from Dalhu's rage. But right now, getting away from him seemed like the smart thing to do.

The roar that left Dalhu's chest shook the cabin, and as she ducked under the comforter, she felt the cabin rattle again when he punched a wall —probably reducing it to dust by the sound of it.

A moment later, she heard the front door open and slam shut.

For long moments, Amanda lay huddled under the blanket, trembling as she listened to every tiny sound.

There were the chirps of crickets and the occasional hoot of an owl, and when the wind picked up, the rustle of leaves and branches swaying and rubbing against each other, but thankfully, no sounds of a madman stomping up the wooden porch steps.

What have I done?

This had been such an incredibly stupid idea. Who in their right mind told their abductor something that they knew would enrage him?

And to what end?

Like having sex with the guy would have been so bad... not! And who cared if she added him to her long list of partners.

As if one more would make a difference...

Though she had a feeling that this one would.

Big time.

Terrified, she waited for Dalhu to come back, fighting to stay awake until exhaustion won the battle.

CHAPTER 6: DALHU

As he stormed out of the cabin, Dalhu didn't know what to do with himself or the rage consuming him. The familiar red haze was clouding his mind. Luckily, trained soldier that he was, he still had enough presence of mind to pull on his boots and then grab a knife and a gun from under the porch floorboards where he'd hidden his weapons.

Who knew what was hiding in this forest? As strong as he was, Dalhu was no match for a full-grown bear, and a pack of coyotes could inflict some serious damage.

On the one hand, he craved the confrontation. A brutal, hands-on fight against vicious beasts would be a great catharsis—a shortcut to getting rid of the raging storm inside his head. But on the other, he couldn't afford an injury. On the remote chance that Amanda's family or his own brethren were to locate them somehow, he needed to conserve his strength to fight them off, or at least give it all he had until they killed him. He wouldn't go down easy.

Unfortunately, he needed to find another way to work out his rage.

Crushing through the forest like an angry grizzly, it took him hours until his head cleared enough for him to think about what had gotten him so enraged.

He didn't know immortal females had a sex drive to match the males. How could he? They were as rare and mysterious as unicorns or honest politicians.

And why the hell had he gotten so mad? It's not like he was a blushing virgin, or even someone who had treated his own body with enough respect not to share it with hell only knew how many goddamned whores…

But that was the thing. He wanted a fresh start with Amanda—to forget what came before and start clean with someone he'd believed was purer.

It's not that he had any illusions about Amanda being a virgin, but to hear her say she'd been with a shitload of men was on a whole different level.

It had shattered his romantic fantasy.

Yeah, he was so goddamned romantic that his woman was terrified of him. Not that he could blame her. He had scared himself. Never in his life had he raised his hand to a woman, but he'd been too damn close to having done it tonight.

And for what? For admitting a truth that had nothing to do with him?

A truth about a physiology he was well familiar with and knew was impossible to deny.

He needed to go back and apologize.

Fuck, he shouldn't have left her alone in the first place—locking her in the cabin.

What if there was a fire and she was trapped inside?

Panic flaring to a bone-melting fear, Dalhu ran, his progress faster and easier on the path that he'd cleared trampling down the mountain before, even though he was going uphill this time.

As he got nearer and detected no smell of smoke, the vise around his heart eased, and as he got to the cabin's front door, he offered a prayer of thanks that nothing had happened to Amanda while he was gone.

It would never happen again.

Nothing was more important than Amanda,

and he'd never allow his goddamned temper or anything else to jeopardize her safety.

Dalhu returned his weapons to their hiding place and took off his soiled boots. Leaving them out on the porch, he manipulated the lock with a few turns of the wire to get back inside.

Careful to close the door soundlessly behind him, he locked it, then tiptoed to the couch. Hopefully, Amanda was asleep, and he was too ashamed of himself to risk going upstairs for a change of clothes and waking her, having to face her. Instead, he dropped his dirty sweats on the floor and lay down, covering his naked body with the thin blanket Amanda had left for him.

But despite his physical and mental exhaustion, sleep eluded him as his thoughts kept running in circles.

He was failing miserably at this whole being a good mate thing. And to think he'd been so sure it would be easy—taking good care of Amanda, providing for her, keeping her safe.

He'd failed on all fronts on the first day.

She didn't have anything good to eat, nothing decent to wear, and he'd gotten her so terrified, he wasn't sure he would ever be able to make her feel safe with him again.

Who was he kidding—as if she ever had—him kidnapping her and all…

Then, he'd left her alone in a locked wooden structure, with no one around to come to her rescue if something went wrong.

He didn't deserve her.

Of course, he didn't.

But he'd make sure to do better tomorrow.

Because failure was not an option.

CHAPTER 7: SHARIM

*A*s Sharim emerged from the underground tunnel, the bright tropical sun blinded him momentarily before he swung the Range Rover to the left, where palm trees shaded the road. Slowing down, he leaned over to the glove compartment and pulled out his sunglasses.

Why, in the name of Mortdh, had his father chosen to live above ground?

The fucking tropical island was relentlessly hot and humid—the sun glaring without mercy day in and day out, all year round. Living in the underground complex on the other side of the island made so much more sense. No sun, no heat, no humidity. Perfect climate control twenty-four seven.

He didn't believe for a moment that his father

chose to live topside because he loved the vivid green of the tropical vegetation and the magnificent view of the ocean, which was Losham's official excuse.

Sharim knew better.

Living in the plush villa adjacent to Navuh's mansion symbolized Losham's elevated status as their supreme leader's eldest son. And to live in the underground facility among the rest of the troops would have undermined his position, even though he would've been residing in the luxurious family wing.

In a way, it was stupid. Navuh's other sons had villas in the luxury resort as well, but for obvious reasons still spent most of their time in the underground. It was a lot more comfortable, not to mention necessary for keeping close tabs on the soldiers.

But his father wasn't a military commander like the others. He wasn't a soldier at all. His main function was providing Navuh with an affable companion.

Soft-spoken and intelligent, Losham managed to appear as if he held some sway with their exalted leader, and maybe to some small extent he did, but the truth was that he was nothing more than a lackey.

Nevertheless, Losham's lofty aspiration had saved Sharim from becoming just another meaningless cog in Navuh's machine, prompting Losham to adopt Sharim as a way to further differentiate himself from Navuh's other sons—Losham's younger half brothers.

Praise Mortdh.

Besides Navuh, none of the other immortal males was allowed to father immortal sons. With Dormants being forbidden to them, the children they sired on mortal females were only mortal.

Sharim had been born to Losham's dormant sister—*the fucking bitch may she burn in hell.*

With some clever groveling, his father had gotten Navuh's permission to adopt Sharim—regrettably, though, only once Sharim was old enough to be taken to the training camp.

Sharim must've been the only boy who'd found living conditions in the camp to be a huge improvement over what he'd been used to in the Dormants' harem.

His mother—*the bitch may she burn in hell*—had hated him with rabid ferocity even before his birth, and it had taken the combined strength of five females to drag her away from the bucket she was trying to drown him in immediately thereafter.

Or so he'd been told.

But considering the way she'd treated him whenever she could put her hands on him, he had no reason to doubt the story.

He'd grown up sleeping in different nooks and crannies and eating scraps from the garbage. Not because the cooks hadn't wanted to feed him, and not because he hadn't been offered a bed to sleep in, but because whenever his bitch of a mother had found him, she'd made sure to let him know just how much she'd hated and despised him.

It had been a miracle he'd survived his mortal childhood to reach the age of transition, and getting there without any permanent deformities had been even a greater miracle. She must've broken nearly every bone in his body...

More than once...

Later, when he was old enough to put one and one together, he'd understood the why.

Not that that understanding had led to forgiveness.

Never.

The bitch had been Navuh's daughter, but unlike her brother Losham and her other half brothers who'd been turned immortal and become leaders, she'd been cast into a whorehouse, relegated to mortality and to serving mortal men with her body for as long as she had remained fertile.

Navuh's daughter hadn't accepted her fate as meekly as the other Dormants. She'd fought off every client, biting and scratching and kicking until overpowered. Consequently, she'd been assigned to males who relished beating and raping her. But though there was never a shortage of those, she'd needed weeks to heal after each assignation before being presentable enough to service the next client, which was probably why she'd only conceived once.

Bless the holy Mortdh.

Parking in his father's driveway, Sharim left his jeep in front of the entry, ascended the three wide steps leading up to the front door, and rang the bell.

One of his father's whores opened the door, her bright, welcoming smile turning into an involuntary cringe when she saw him. She recovered quickly, though, plastering a fake smile on her face. "Greetings, master." She inclined her head. "Please come in. Your father awaits."

Sharim smiled back, committing her features to memory. She was safe for as long as his father kept her around, but eventually Losham would tire of her and send her back.

Sharim would pay her a visit then.

Losham didn't share his son's sadistic proclivities, and after the one time he'd offered Sharim the use of one of his whores, he had never done it again.

Couldn't stomach the screams.

His father was such a soft male.

After all, it wasn't as if Sharim was inflicting permanent damage on the merchandise. The venom healed the bruises and welts in two days tops, and he was always careful not to break any bones or injure any internal organs. That kind of damage took much longer to heal, and he didn't want to be held accountable for all the lost profits from the time it took the whores to recover.

Compared to what his own mother had done to him, Sharim was tender...

Walking behind the whore, his eyes followed her swaying ass. With the two pale cheeks separated only by a narrow strip of red bikini and bouncing enticingly with each of her steps, he imagined adorning them with a different kind of red stripes—crisscrossing the welts—his cane striking mercilessly as she screamed and begged for mercy...

Mercy that he wasn't going to grant.

Whoa... He had to rein himself in.

To greet his father with dripping fangs and a hard-on would be a total lack of decorum...

Digging his nails into his palms hard enough to draw blood, he shifted his eyes away from that enticing ass and focused on the light reflecting from his shiny Dolce & Gabbana loafers.

As the whore pushed through the double doors to his father's study, Sharim wasn't surprised to find the guy seated on the couch with a pretty girl on each side.

"Good morning, Father." Sharim bowed his head a little.

"Come in, son." Losham kissed each pretty on the mouth before gently pushing them up. "Go, have some fun in the pool, girls." He got up and ushered the three out, closing and locking the doors behind them.

This is strange...

Why lock the doors?

"Let's play some chess." His father motioned to the table he'd dedicated to the game.

As always, the beautiful black and white ivory pieces were set up and ready for a new game, and Sharim took his place at the white army's side. His father, a true chess master, always insisted Sharim should have the advantage of making the first move.

Losham poured them each a shot of Macallan whiskey, and handing Sharim his glass, sat across from him in front of the black.

"I was surprised at your summons today, Father. Our game night was just a couple of evenings ago. May I assume you have more than chess on your mind?" Sharim pushed a pawn up.

"Naturally, but why waste an opportunity. It is always an exciting challenge to play against you, Sharim. You're a worthy opponent."

"Yet, you win every time."

"Yes, but it's getting harder. One of these days you are going to best me. And I think sooner rather than later."

"Thank you, I appreciate your confidence in my ability, but I'm afraid it would take another century or two for me to finally win, if ever. You've been winning for a millennium. Nothing has changed."

"Well, this is not entirely true. The name of the game has changed. It used to be Shatranj. Remember?"

"Certainly." Sharim waited patiently for his father to get to the real reason behind the meeting.

Losham made his move and leaned back in his chair. "I am sure you are aware of the success reported by our team in America, yes?"

"Of course."

"In light of his spectacular achievement, eliminating one of our enemies' main assets, the leader of the team requests reinforcements. He wants to go hunting for more of Annani's clan members."

"Yes, I'm well aware of that. But what does it have to do with me? Surely you don't think this kind of mission requires someone of my caliber..."

"Actually, I do. Dalhu got lucky. But this is above his pay grade. And besides, I have more in mind than a simple hunt." Losham smiled.

"Go on..."

"As you know, since the beginning, we have been using two main tactics in our war against Annani and her clan. The first was to support the enemies of her Western allies—those who didn't get to benefit from her stolen knowledge and envied those who did, eager to destroy them. The second was to sow seeds of destruction from the inside, nurturing them with clever propaganda until they grew and multiplied, eating up and destroying from within all of the progress previously achieved. Like we did in WWI and WWII, and many other smaller implosions."

Nothing new here, Sharim thought as he nodded, waiting to see where his father was leading with this simplified rehashing of their age-old strategies.

"But we have never been able to do it to the Americans. Unhindered, they had become the main power to contend with. Lately, though, it seems that the clever Americans lost some of their acuity, letting weeds of their own take root and grow unchecked. They are weakened from the inside; taking away resources from their armed forces and abandoning allies to various bullies around the world..."

Now it's getting interesting... Sharim edged closer to the table.

Losham continued, "The Americans losing their leadership position provides us with an amazing opportunity. If we help accelerate that trend, we will achieve WWIII in no time. Without the United States to protect it, the West is up for grabs. The various power-hungry crazies around the world are already raising their heads and are poised to destroy all the progressive, technologically advanced countries that would be left defenseless with no armies of their own to speak of. The world would revert to the dark ages." Losham's intelligent eyes shone with excitement as he waited for Sharim to make his move.

Sharim ventured with his knight though his

mind wasn't on the chessboard anymore. It was now on the larger game at hand.

Losham was obviously letting himself get carried away on the wings of wishful thinking and his own imagination. The United States was still the strongest nation in the world, with the largest, most powerful army, and it would take a lot more than what his father was describing to weaken it. Still, planting weeds in that fertile soil was always a good strategy. One had to be careful about it, though. A few weeds here and there that grew hidden from watchful eyes and undermined the strong foundation that country was built on were a better strategy than planting whole fields of them and attracting the watchers' attention.

"How do you propose we do it?"

"It is so easy, it is laughable. I do not even need to come up with creative ideas. They did it all for me. All we need to hasten their downfall is a gentle shove."

"I'm listening."

"Do you know why most of the European countries face bankruptcy despite their technology and their lofty democratic ideas?"

Sharim nodded, at the last moment refraining from snorting. "Everyone knows. Not enough people in the workforce to finance runaway government spending."

"Well, apparently not everyone knows because the United States is heading in the same direction. Unreasonable regulation and taxation drive businesses to take their production abroad. Fewer and fewer jobs are available for Americans, more and more people are forced to rely on welfare, and no money is left to keep armed forces that are formidable enough to act as a deterrent to the various upstarts."

"So why do we need to do anything? With the trajectory they are on, their downfall is inevitable."

A cunning smile tugging at his lips, Losham braced his elbows on the table and steepled his fingers. "Yes, but we need to make sure they stay on that path. They could still turn things around. American workers are the most productive in the world, followed by the Germans and the Scandinavians. Their productivity keeps their economies from collapsing despite the excessive regulation and taxation. For now."

He took a sip from his glass before continuing.

"So here is what I want you to do. Besides taking charge of the hunt, that is. You will start working on their media and their movie industry while your counterpart will work on Washington."

"I thought we were already doing that."

"Yes, but we did it in an indirect way, providing funds to organizations that supported our agenda, financing those student organizations in their learning institutions who voiced the views we wanted them to, providing the environmentalists with shitloads of money for their campaigns and their lobbyists, etc. The results are fantastic, by far exceeding our best case expectations."

Losham chuckled. "It is absolutely amazing how gullible people are. Where do they think the environmentalists get the money to pay for their campaigns and finance their lobbyists? The trees? No one stops to think that whoever is providing that much money expects to profit from their investment. If anyone did, they would follow the logic, put two and two together, and figure out who it is that stands to gain the most from its success. How come no one is crying out about the meat industry and its impact on the environment? Cows cause as much pollution as cars and yet no one is trying to persuade people to stop eating meat. Why? Because no one stands to gain anything from it while a big and powerful industry stands to lose a lot. Besides, it puts responsibility on the individual, and most people are not willing to give up their steaks and their hamburgers for the environment.

Sharim chuckled. "You're right. Truth be told, I had no idea livestock is responsible for this much pollution."

"All it takes is a quick Internet search. But I guess Global Warming sounds a lot sexier than cows and their waste products."

"When you suggested we jump on the whole global-warming thing, I was afraid our allies would be negatively impacted because alternative sources of energy will mean less fossil fuel sales for them. But it seems I had nothing to fear." Sharim lifted his glass in salute.

"That was the beauty of my plan. Who would ever suspect the biggest oil producers of funding an environmental agenda? Ha? But you see, son, you hadn't thought the whole thing through the way I did. People still want to drive their cars and use electricity, and factories need to produce. So even if everyone did their best to conserve, the population of the world still keeps growing, and consumption is growing with it. They have to get the energy somewhere. But thanks to all the environmental brouhaha, there is no drilling for oil to speak of in the West, and no new nuclear power generation either. Guess who they need to keep buying from?"

Sharim regarded his father with newfound appreciation.

Losham sighed. "The thing is, the big gears are moving, but not fast enough. Lord Navuh is getting impatient. He wants to quicken the pace."

"How?"

"On one front, by threatening and blackmailing anyone who is voicing opposition to the current policy, and publicly demonizing those that we cannot get to. On another, by pushing for more and more regulation to choke up their industry, so more of it will be forced to move out to third-world countries to remain competitive. This will result in even fewer jobs for Americans. I want you to buy TV stations, cable stations, movie production companies, and controlling interest in news publications. We need to keep the American public's focus away from the storm of shit that is stinking up the rest of the world and heading their way."

Losham finished the last of his whiskey and got up to refill their glasses.

"I know I am asking a lot from you, son. But if anyone can pull it off without leaving a trail that can lead back to us, it is you. You have done it successfully before."

"What's my budget?"

"Basically unlimited. Lord Navuh is a hundred percent behind this, as are our deep-pocketed allies."

"I must say, I'm impressed with the scope of this campaign, and tremendously flattered to be one of the two entrusted with leading it."

"My part was the long term planning and assigning the right men to implement it. The rest is up to you and your counterpart in Washington. I've been teaching you and grooming you for over a thousand years, and you're more than ready, my boy. The logistics and all the rest of the planning minutiae I leave to you."

Sharim pushed up from his chair, and as his father offered him his palm, he bowed and kissed the back of Losham's hand in a show of utmost respect.

"I will not disappoint you, Father."

"I know, my son." Losham pulled him into an embrace.

With his head buzzing with all he'd learned, Sharim got into his jeep and drove back to the base, his plans for spending some pleasant time in the whorehouse completely forgotten.

What a disrespectful fool he'd been for thinking his father was just a yes man for Navuh.

Losham was absolutely brilliant, and apparently Lord Navuh was well aware of the fact, keeping his eldest son at his side not because the man was a pleasant, agreeable companion, but because he was a great strategist.

And such modesty.

Thinking of the few times he'd alluded to his father's unimportant position in the organization, Sharim cringed. Losham had never bothered to correct him, smiling as if agreeing with the misguided perception, when, in fact, he was the one making all those smart plans in their exalted leader's name.

"Checkmate, Father. You win again." Sharim saluted as his headlights turned on, illuminating the dark tunnel leading back to the base.

He was so proud of his father...

So proud to be Losham's son.

CHAPTER 8: AMANDA

With the morning's diffused sunshine warming her face, Amanda reluctantly opened her eyes and shifted to her back. The light was coming through the only windows that weren't shuttered, the two small glass triangles flanking the cabin's stone fireplace at its top. Looking out, all she could see were green treetops swaying gently against the cloudless, blue background.

It was a beautiful day.

Somewhere in the mountains…

So yesterday wasn't a bad dream. She really got kidnapped by an insane, huge Doomer, who initially had wanted her for his mate, but owing to her monumental stupidity had probably changed his mind and was going to kill her instead.

The good news was that Dalhu hadn't come back to chop off her head.

Yet…

And perhaps, if luck would have it, he wouldn't come back at all…

So why did she feel a ping of regret at the prospect of never seeing him again?

Because she was an idiot, who had the hots for a Doomer.

And to think that she'd actually started to like the brute. In a way, it was good that she'd discovered his true nature before doing something she would've regretted later. Not that doing the something that she had in mind with Dalhu would've been okay under any circumstances.

Luckily, it was off the table now. Hot or not, the guy was a ticking time bomb.

Scooting to the foot of the bed, she lifted to her knees and took a peek over the railing.

Shit.

Dalhu was sleeping on the couch with his long legs hanging over the armrest, one muscular arm resting on the couch's back, the other hanging down its side.

Naked.

Magnificent.

Unfortunately, the blanket covering his midsection robbed her of a full frontal view.

Bummer.

You are an idiot, Amanda.

This man, as mouth-watering as he was, was a killer.

With a sigh, she tore her eyes away from all that maleness, grabbed her purse, and tiptoed to the bathroom.

One look at the vanity mirror and her mood plummeted even lower. She looked just as awful as she felt. Or perhaps worse. There were dark circles under her eyes that had nothing to do with the black mascara smudges, her hair was a messed-up jungle and not half as glossy as it usually was after shampooing and conditioning with her custom-formulated hair products, and the pink sweats she was wearing were absolutely hideous.

Looking horrible, in addition to having a homicidal lunatic sleeping down on the couch, was utterly depressing.

Amanda sighed. There was nothing to be done about the pink polyester monstrosity, but she could do something about the hair and the face. Splashing cold water on her head helped to tame the wild mess into something manageable, and she felt a little better after washing her face and applying makeup.

Trouble was, once done with her morning routine, there was nothing to distract her from how parched she was or how empty her stomach felt. Going down to the kitchen, though, risked rousing the angry bear on the couch.

Another trip to the bathroom took care of the thirst problem. Though blah... drinking water from the faucet was a new low for her. Still, there was the issue of her growling tummy. A quick search through her purse yielded nothing edible—unless one counted the cherry-flavored lip gloss.

Oh, what the hell.

Slinking down the stairs, she did her best to avoid making any noise, putting as little weight as possible on the wooden stairs and bracing most of it on the wall-side railing.

She made it all the way down without waking Dalhu, but then couldn't resist getting a little closer for a better look.

Big mistake.

With him being so yummy, and her being so hungry—and not strictly for food—she had to shove a fist into her mouth and bite it to stifle the involuntary moan.

You're such a stupid slut, Amanda! Inching back, she turned around and tiptoed into the kitchen.

Another peanut butter sandwich coming up. Yippiee ki-yay.

Her cardboard-tasting creation in hand, Amanda leaned against the counter and eyed the cold pot of coffee Dalhu had made last night. But even though it was right there on the stove, she didn't dare heat it up. Turning on the electric stove would be soundless, but the boiling water was sure to make some noise. Even she knew as much.

Oh, hell. Old, cold coffee is better than none. Right?

Or maybe not.

The stuff tasted like mud. Not that she'd ever eaten dirt before... but if it quacked like a duck, it probably tasted like one too, and all that...

"I'll make you a new one." Dalhu's deep voice had her whip around so fast that she got dizzy and listed to the side, putting a hand out to steady herself.

In a flash, he was right next to her, propping her up by her elbow. "Easy there, girl."

Her heart up in her throat, Amanda scooted away and wedged herself into a corner of cabinets. Not that it offered any real shelter, but with Dalhu blocking the way she had nowhere to go.

He didn't move a muscle. Standing near the

sink and clutching the blanket he wore like a sarong around his hips, he looked at her with dark, sorrowful eyes. "Please, Amanda, don't be afraid of me. I would never, ever, hurt you. I swear."

"Could've fooled me. Just take a look at the poor wall you took your anger out on. You demolished half of it with your bare fist." She motioned to the gaping hole in the wall across from the fridge. "I'm just glad it wasn't my face."

Dalhu winced. "I'm sorry. So sorry that I got angry. But I would've never raised my hand to you. You must believe that. You have nothing to fear. Walls, on the other hand, are a different story." He attempted a smile.

"The mindless beast that you turned into wasn't doing much thinking. You were completely out of control. After you left, I hid under the blanket for hours, afraid to fall asleep, just waiting for you to come back and chop off my head..." The expression of horror contorting his face stopped her mid-rant.

"Never! Oh, hell, Amanda, I would rather die a thousand horrible deaths than hurt you. You must believe me..." He reached for her cheek, but she flinched away.

"I'm so sorry." Dalhu let his hand drop by his side. "I'm going to get dressed. When I come back,

I'll make you a new pot of coffee." He spun around and headed for the stairs.

Amanda remained glued to her spot until she heard the bathroom's floorboards squeak under Dalhu's weight. Releasing a relieved breath, she pushed away from the corner and with a shaky hand lifted her abandoned sandwich.

Unfortunately, as much as Amanda wanted to believe him, she couldn't trust Dalhu's promises. He might've meant each and every one, but then his intentions were not the problem.

The big question was whether his higher reasoning functioned at all when he raged. Unbalanced and combustive, he was like a stick of dynamite. She figured it wouldn't take more than a tiny spark to ignite him. And like the explosive, Dalhu wouldn't discriminate about what got caught in his circle of destruction.

Still, explosive or not, the man sure as hell was dynamite-hot, Amanda thought as Dalhu came down to the kitchen looking like a model from GQ magazine in a pair of Balmain jeans and a Tom Ford button-down. Not that he didn't look amazing with nothing more than a blanket tied around his hips, but damn... it was her turn to do a little drooling.

Except, where the hell did he get that designer

getup? She frowned. "You certainly cleaned up nicely. Question is, how is it that you get to wear fancy stuff while I'm wearing cheap, butt-ugly sweats?" Indignation overriding trepidation, Amanda placed her hands on her hips and began tapping her bare foot on the linoleum floor.

"Everything is dirty, and I have nothing to wear aside from these faggot clothes. And the only reason I have this shit with me in the first place is that I'd been shopping for an appropriate attire to wear to an exclusive club when I got sidetracked by my dream girl. But once the laundry is done, we can both go back to wearing what we had on yesterday."

"Don't get me wrong, you look very nice... not gayish at all, very manly in fact... Wait a second, what was that about laundry? Don't tell me you put my things in the washer!"

"Why? What's the problem? I know how to use one."

"My clothes are dry-clean only, you stupid man. You ruined them!" Amanda threw her hands in the air. "Where is that thing? Maybe I can still salvage something."

Dalhu didn't respond. Instead, he glared at her with a murderous expression on his face—his silence as loud and as terrifying as the worst of thunderstorms.

Oh, boy, I did it again, didn't I.

"I'm so sorry. You're not stupid. Really... it's just an expression. Please don't kill me..." Cringing, she backed into the corner again.

CHAPTER 9: DALHU

What the hell was she apologizing for? He was the one that had failed her yet again, ruining her clothes. Would he ever do anything right for this woman? He'd thought it would be a nice surprise, getting her things clean so she could go back to wearing her fancy clothes. How was he supposed to know that her stuff wasn't washable? It wasn't as if he had ever done a woman's laundry before...

And what the fuck was the "please don't kill me" about?

"I'm the one who should be apologizing for ruining your things, not you, and I'm angry with myself, not you. But you've got to stop that cowering routine you got going on because *that* really pisses me off." Dalhu drew in a calming breath and hung his head. "And you are absolutely right. I'm stupid and incompetent. I want to take good care of you, but instead, I keep failing time and again."

He waited for the longest moment for Amanda to say something.

She didn't. Not even when she moved out of that damned corner, walked over to the dining table and plopped down on a chair.

Sitting as she did with her back to him, he couldn't see her face. Was she angry? Sad? Should he go to her? Leave her alone to stew?

But then her shoulders began heaving.

Oh, hell.

He rushed to her side, but she wasn't crying.

Soon, what had started as a soft chuckle turned into a bubbling laugh, her whole body shaking with it.

What the fuck?

Did she really think any of this was funny?

Or perhaps it was some form of hysterics, and any moment now her laughter would turn into sobs.

But as she kept at it, laughing and wiping the tears away with the sleeves of her sweatshirt, he got caught up in her madness and joined in, laughing so hard he had to sit down because he got a stitch in his side.

Dalhu couldn't remember the last time he'd laughed so hard, and it felt foreign—like a language he'd once known, but had forgotten. The sounds were familiar, but he found it difficult to form them in his throat, his mouth...

"Oh, Dalhu, what a mismatched pair we are," Amanda croaked once she caught her breath. "Yin and yang. Black and white. What are we going to do?" She regarded him warily, her eyes saying the things she was afraid to voice.

The same arguments she had from the start. That there was no way to bridge the differences between them. That there was no real chance for them to find common ground. That he was deluding himself if he thought they could build a life together.

But what she failed to understand was that he'd never give up, never stop trying. That he might fail over and over again, but in time he'd learn. And as he had all the time in the world for all the do-overs ever needed, in the end, he'd prevail.

If he'd learned one lesson in his long life, it was that perseverance was the key to success. It wasn't the smartest or the most talented who rose to positions of power, in business as well as in politics or even in the military—it was the one who kept pushing. The earth would not be inherited by the meek, and not even by those born with the advantage of superior intelligence or physical attributes. The earth was ruled by those who worked relentlessly toward achieving their goals, those who always got up after falling, those who never accepted defeat.

Like him.

Dalhu got to his feet and walked over to the other side of the table to stand beside her. "What we're going to do is talk, a lot. We are going to ask questions and get to know each other. But first, I'm going to make us a fresh pot of coffee and something to eat."

Gazing up at him, Amanda's huge blue eyes were red-rimmed from her tears, and her dark makeup was smeared all over her face. And still, the woman was a vision.

"It will be all right. You'll see." He smoothed her short, glossy hair with his palm. Bending down, he kissed her forehead, not trusting himself to kiss her lips again.

"Yeah, if you don't kill me first…" He heard her murmur under her breath as he moved over to the stove.

"Would you stop that already?" he grated as he

dumped the old coffee in the sink.

The excessive force he'd used caused the dark slosh to splatter, getting all over the cabinets and staining his brand new, six-hundred-dollar shirt.

As a veil of red clouded his vision, Dalhu felt a roar pushing up from his gut.

That was it.

He couldn't take it anymore. He was going to explode.

The built-up pressure was seeking release, and it would just blow out of the top of his head and put an end to his misery.

A crazed chuckle escaped his throat as he thought of the irony of surviving countless battles only to be done in by a cold pot of coffee.

No.

Not again.

He couldn't explode like a fucking madman and terrify Amanda. He had to fight the rage. Dalhu gripped the edge of the sink with such force that the tiles under his fingers began crumbling.

"Breathe, Dalhu. It's okay. It's only a shirt. If you take it off, I'll wash it right away, and there'll be no stains."

The effect of Amanda's calm voice, combined with the feel of her delicate hand going up and down over the knotted muscles of his back was—

for lack of a better word—miraculous. Like a gentle wave of cool water, it washed over the raging inferno consuming him, putting the fire out and soothing his raw nerves.

Dalhu closed his eyes and breathed in long and hard before letting the air back out, then did it again until his breathing evened out.

"Better?" Amanda asked quietly, her hand never ceasing its soothing up and down trek on his back.

"Yes, thank you," he breathed just as quietly.

"Is it okay if I wash your shirt now?"

"Yes." Dalhu spun around, facing Amanda, but that was as far as he was able to go. If she wanted his shirt, she'd have to take it off herself.

She peered up at him with worry in her big eyes. "Are you sure you're okay? You look a little dazed. Maybe you should sit down."

"No, I'm fine. I just need a moment…"

"Okay, big guy. Take your time." Amanda reached for the first button, then paused, waiting for his assent.

"Please." He nodded.

Going slowly, as if afraid to spook a wild animal, Amanda unbuttoned his shirt. She then spread the two halves and pushed it down his shoulders until he finally helped her by shrugging it off.

"I'll take it up to the bathroom and wash it there. You just take your time." Amanda dropped her eyes to the shirt she was holding and eased back.

"Wait..." Dalhu caught her arm. "Please, I need to feel your hand on me again." She regarded him quizzically, but didn't resist as he took her palm and placed it on his bare skin, right over where his heart was still hammering a crazy beat.

The effect was immediate, with that soothing calm washing over him once again. "You're an angel..." he breathed in awe, holding his palm over her hand and keeping it on him for as long as she would let him.

"I think you're a little confused... delirious. But thank you." Amanda blushed prettily.

What a strange and wonderful creature she was. An innocent compliment made her blush while talking about her numerous lovers left her completely unaffected. "I called you an angel because what you've been able to do for me is nothing short of a miracle."

"I'm glad. Now let me go before this shirt is a goner." She tried to pull away.

"Fuck the shirt... I'm sorry. I shouldn't use foul language around you."

"Don't be ridiculous, Dalhu. Stop trying so hard

and just relax. I'm really not an angel, and a fuck here and there doesn't offend me—" She stopped and slapped a hand over her mouth, a shadow of fear crossing her eyes.

He chuckled. "It's okay. I'm over the shocking newsflash that immortal females have a healthy sex appetite to match that of their males. And I'm starting to get your twisted sense of humor as well. In fact, I love it." He closed his fingers over the hand she was covering her mouth with and lifted it to his lips for a light kiss. "I want you to feel free to say whatever is on your mind. Always. And if I get angry, again... Well, we have the antidote. All you need to do is touch me..."

"You sure? I have a really big mouth, and it has no filter."

"Positive."

"In that case... how long do I have to wait for a cup of coffee around here? I'm telling you, the service in this establishment is just subpar..." She winked.

Reluctantly, he let go of her hands. "It is, isn't it?"

"Well, get on it, big guy."

"Yes, ma'am."

CHAPTER 10: SHARIM

*B*y nightfall, Sharim had his two lieutenants and an administrative assistant for the mission selected. From the troop under his command, he'd chosen seventy-two of his best warriors.

Unlike the other commanders, who led by fear and intimidation, Sharim treated his men well and thus earned their loyalty. He spent time with them, knew each one by name and temperament, and knew exactly what could be expected from whom.

Those who knew him as a commander had a hard time believing that he was a self-proclaimed sadist and proud of it. Not surprisingly, they couldn't reconcile the charming, soft-spoken guy with someone who loved inflicting pain on others. Well, women in particular. Though, if needed, he had no problem torturing males for information. It just didn't turn him on.

Besides, he believed that if one was smart, one didn't mix business with pleasure, and what he did for sex during his free time had no bearing on his job.

Which brought his train of thought to the issue of scheduling a scene for tonight. After all that good work, he was in an exceptionally good mood —excited and full of energy. Hence, instead of selecting one of the newbies, he decided to call for the one hooker that actually enjoyed his kind of attention.

A quick text and he had it arranged. Once he was done in the office, Marla would be waiting for him, kneeling naked by the door the way he liked. After all, there were some advantages to dealing with an experienced sub—one who was well familiar with his particular preferences—instead of torturing some uninitiated tart...

Good, good, good... Sharim rubbed his hands and went over his list again.

It had been a productive day. An excellent utilization of time and resources—if he may say so himself.

After explaining how he wanted to go about it,

Sharim had assigned the task of arranging the elaborate travel plans to his assistant.

There would be no more traveling in groups.

He had been appalled when he'd seen the travel arrangements for the small unit that had uncovered the clan's American location. They had been extremely lucky that airport security had not tagged them as suspects. Three groups of four men in the span of only two days. The least they could have done was to divide the groups unevenly. But this was what happened when travel arrangements were left to low-level bureaucrats.

The administrative branch of their army consisted of the least capable personnel, those who'd been deemed too inferior to be warriors. The best way to utilize their meager capabilities was to provide them with clear and precise step-by-step instructions. But apparently Dalhu, the leader of that group, had failed to do so.

Well, not really the guy's fault. An organization should keep examining and reexamining its procedures and install new ones when something didn't work as smoothly as it should. He would e-mail the head of that department and suggest that a new procedure be put in place for every commander to follow upon traveling on an assignment to the

West. And just to be clear, he'd include his own clever travel plans as a blueprint.

Once the island's transport plane dropped them off at Kuala Lumpur, Malaysia, each man would fly to a different destination in the world, going through at least two other countries with a different fake passport for each leg of the trip before arriving at Los Angeles International Airport.

Sharim, one of his lieutenants, and his personal assistant would leave tomorrow morning. The zigzag route that he had planned for them would get them to their final destination in about seventy-two hours.

Starting two weeks later, the rest of the men would follow, trickling in over a period of several days.

He'd have plenty of time to take care of the rest of the logistics en route and then once he got to Los Angeles.

First and foremost on his agenda was securing a suitable place for a base and arranging for weapons and other supplies to be purchased and delivered for when the men arrived. The modifications and fortifications could be done while the men were already there, but the perimeter had to be secured with a proper fence and surveillance equipment beforehand.

With a few phone calls to the Brotherhood's contacts in Los Angeles, he'd arranged a search for appropriate properties—the promise of a five-figure cash commission and a bonus for fast delivery lighting a fire under the two Realtors' butts.

Hopefully, by tomorrow there would be some good properties lined up for him, and he'd be able to close a deal before reaching his next stop.

CHAPTER 11: AMANDA

Check me out, playing house, like a good little woman...

Amanda hung the shirt she'd washed by hand on the shower curtain rod.

But what the hell, if Dalhu could cook and do laundry, she could deign to wash one shirt. And anyway, she was quite satisfied with herself for getting all the stains out.

Judging by the enticing smells coming from the kitchen, coffee was ready and Dalhu was cooking something that smelled pretty good. Unfortunately, being the one who'd unpacked their supplies, she was well aware of what he had to work with and doubted that she'd find the end product of his efforts edible.

If that man wasn't planning to starve her, he

really needed to go shopping. And if she didn't want a repeat of the general store fiasco, she'd better make him a detailed list.

Amanda pulled a pen out of her purse and, for lack of other options, tore a big piece off one of the brown paper bags from the general store Dalhu had robbed.

Well, he did leave some money to cover the cost of what he took.

Wasted his money was more like it. It was all the worst quality of junk. As soon as he delivered the new supplies, she'd have him throw out all that stuff.

Everything except the pink monstrosity she was wearing.

That, she would burn and dance a victory dance around the fire. Though with all its polyester content, she wasn't sure if it would burn or melt.

"Breakfast is ready!" Dalhu called from the kitchen.

"Coming!"

Well, I wish I were... Naughty, naughty Amanda. Put a brake on your one-track mind...

Holding her pen and a piece of the brown paper bag, she jogged down the stairs.

Dalhu had the table set with two plates heaped

with something unrecognizable and two cups of coffee... one already whitened with the condensed milk.

"Thank you," she said as she sat down next to where he'd placed it.

"You are welcome. I hope you like it." Dalhu smiled and sat across from her.

Amanda moved things around her plate with the fork, trying to guess what was in the weird mush. "You know how you said I should say whatever I want?"

"Yes. What's the matter? You haven't even tasted it yet..."

"No, I know. It's just that it's a sure thing I'm going to bitch about it, and I thought saying something nice first would be a good idea."

"Okay?" He cocked an eyebrow.

"First, thank you for remembering how I like my coffee, and for making this food, and setting the table, and everything... And for looking real fine without a shirt..."

Dalhu almost choked on what was in his mouth. "Really? Well... you're welcome... and thank you." He barely managed to get the words out. "Now, please, just taste it. It's not as bad as it looks."

"Okay. Here goes..." Amanda lifted a tiny

amount of the slosh with her fork, hesitating before bringing the stuff into her mouth. When it didn't trigger an immediate gag reflex, she gave chewing a try.

Dalhu's eyes were on her mouth, the poor guy forgetting to breathe as he awaited her verdict.

"It's edible. Which considering what you had to work with is an accomplishment. But unless you think I need to lose a lot of weight, you'd better go shopping." She was being generous. The stuff tasted just a tad better than throw-up, but she had no heart to tell him that.

"I don't want you to lose even an ounce. You're perfect the way you are. Make the list and I'll see what I can do. But for now this is all we have, and I don't want you to go hungry until I come back." He motioned to her plate and waited.

She forced herself to take a few forkfuls, washing down each one with generous gulps of coffee, but as soon as Dalhu shifted his attention to his own plate, she got busy making the list.

Taking into consideration that Dalhu had limited experience with shopping, she decided to group the items on her list by store and the department they could be found at. The clothing and undergarments, as well as cosmetics and skincare, were the easiest—she'd shopped for these herself and knew exactly where to get them. After all, it shouldn't matter that she had shopped at Bloomingdales and Saks while Dalhu would be lucky to find a Macy's. One department store shouldn't be all that different from another, at least as far as the configuration went. The rest of the stuff, the things Onidu took care of like bedding and food, she had to guess.

When she was done, the brown piece of paper was covered in her tight, messy script. "My handwriting is really messy. I think I should read it to you. Or better yet, come with you..." She glanced at him hopefully.

"Not a chance, princess, not this time."

"When, then? You can't keep me here forever. I'll go crazy. There is no TV, no Internet, nothing for me to do..."

"I realize that." Dalhu sighed. "I just need a little more time to figure out my next step. It's not like I had this whole thing planned out. And besides, I don't trust you not to run. Yet... I'm sorry."

With a huff, Amanda crossed her arms over her chest. "Well, it was worth a try."

The rest of the meal went by with her glaring at Dalhu and him polishing off both his plate and hers. She didn't offer to help him when he cleared the dishes, washed them, and wiped the table clean.

He didn't deserve it.

Once he was done, he came to stand beside her and offered her a hand up. "Come. Let's see that list."

"I'm mad at you." She shrugged.

"I know. But I'm sure getting the things on that list is more important to you than staying mad at me."

Well, when he put it like that…

She let him pull her up and walk her to the couch, where he had her sit beside him as he tried to decipher her scribbles.

CHAPTER 12: DALHU

*A*manda had no way of knowing that he was already familiar with her peculiar handwriting, and although he planned on telling her everything at some point in the future, that point wasn't now.

He had spent hours with her little notebook, the one his men had found in her lab, learning a lot from it. Her chicken scribbles, as he'd at first referred to her handwriting, were mostly about her research, both the official one that she had done for the university and the unofficial one she'd run on mortals with paranormal abilities. But not only. Between her random ideas and her little drawings he had glimpsed her unique personality, her mischievous streak, her loyalty to her clan, and how much their loneliness, as well as her own, weighed heavily on her.

Granted, it felt wrong to pretend he was having more trouble understanding what she'd written than he actually did, but as the saying went: all was fair in love and battle... or something along those lines.

As it was, though, Amanda must've been out of her mind if she thought he could get everything on her list, or that he even knew what some of the things were...

"Fifteen hundred TC organic Egyptian cotton bed sheets? What the hell does it even mean? Or that Japanese sounding moisturizer thing, Shiseido?"

"It's nothing complicated. Any decent department store will have all of those things. Look, I organized the list by departments; all you need to do is find a Nordstrom or a Bloomingdales or even a Macy's and ask a salesperson in each department to help you."

Was it a trick? A guy like him shopping for stuff like that and asking for help would be hard to forget. Was she planning to leave a trail for those searching for her? But his nose was telling him she was excited but not fearful, which she would have been if she was planning some subterfuge.

"Okay. I'll see what I can do. Let's move to the food list. What does good bread that doesn't taste like cardboard mean? How am I supposed to know which one tastes good to you without a brand name? And other than the bread, all I see is an assortment of cheeses, frozen pizzas, and fruits. Where is the rest of the stuff, like meat and eggs, fresh vegetables?"

"First of all, I'm a vegetarian. I don't eat meat. Second, my expertise at buying food is limited to picking stuff from a restaurant menu. And that goes for cooking as well..." Amanda leaned back and crossed her arms over her chest. "If you wanted someone to cook and clean for you, you certainly picked the wrong girl," she added with a snort.

"No, I wasn't looking for a maid. I was looking for a mate, a partner. I couldn't care less that you're challenged in these areas..." He flashed her a sideways grin.

Her eyes narrowed into slits and she pursed her lips, looking absolutely stunning despite her peeved expression.

Oh, man, did she have any idea what she was doing to him with those lush lips of hers puffed and begging to be kissed? If she didn't, she was soon going to find out.

Quick as a snake, he struck, taking those lips in a hungry kiss. When she didn't resist, he pushed her down on the couch and deepened the kiss, his tongue licking into the sweetness of her mouth.

Amanda moaned, grabbing his shoulders to bring him closer to her chest… Then, with a growl, she gave a strong shove and pushed him off.

Damn, she was strong for a woman. Which shouldn't have surprised him. It made perfect sense that if immortal males were stronger than their human counterparts, so were the females.

Amanda jumped off the couch. Holding the torn piece of paper with her list, she pointed at the door. "You need to get going. I don't know how far you need to drive to get me what I need, so you'd better hurry." She panted, her other hand resting over her racing heart.

"I will, in a moment. First, a little safety talk. I'm not going to lock you in because I don't want to risk you being trapped inside in case of a fire or an earthquake. But I don't want you wandering outside. And I'm not saying this to keep you from trying to escape. We are hours away from civilization and there are wild animals out there. So please, be smart about it and don't leave the cabin, not even to sit on the porch. And don't open the door to get fresh air in either—or any other such bright ideas. I'm serious." He pinned her with a hard stare.

"I got it. No going outside, and no opening the door. Now go…"

"Promise. I want you to swear on it."

Amanda rolled her eyes. "Sheesh! I promise! Swear to Bob and all that… I'm not stupid, you know."

When he still didn't move, she threw her hands in the air. "Men," she muttered under her breath before stomping away and climbing the stairs to the loft.

"I'll be back as soon as I can," he called after her.

Without looking back, she shrugged and then disappeared into the bathroom.

Dalhu almost made it out the door when he remembered he was shirtless.

Going up the stairs, he glanced toward the bathroom door, hoping to get a peek of what she was doing in there, but Amanda had propped something against it to hold it closed.

Damn.

He grabbed another one of the fancy shirts and shrugged it on, buttoning it on his way out.

Out on the porch, he lifted the loose plank and pulled out the car keys and his duffle bag. Not that he needed weapons and ammunition for his acquisition trip, or his laptop, but with Amanda left unsupervised and with plenty of time on her hands, she might get the urge to do some reconnaissance.

CHAPTER 13: AMANDA

*a*s the sun began its slow descent, Amanda got hungry again. But the thought of eating another peanut butter-covered cardboard was motivation enough to endure the hunger pangs for a little longer.

She could wait until Dalhu showed up with something edible.

What the hell was taking him so long? It had been more than six hours since he had left. For his sake, she hoped he'd come back with everything on her list, otherwise... what?

Well, she could ignore him. There wasn't much else she could do. It wasn't as if she could stomp her foot and walk out on him. With a *humph*. Except, being ignored would probably hurt Dalhu enough. The way he was desperate for every little crumb of affection she threw his way…

Poor guy.

Damn, she was hungry. What if he wouldn't be back for hours?

But she really couldn't stomach another sandwich. She'd rather starve.

Then again, maybe she could open a can of corn and another one of beans and mix them together.

Shouldn't be too bad...

Oh, how low the mighty have fallen...

Pulling the two cans down from the upper cupboard, she read the instructions.

Good, it said on the labels that the stuff didn't need cooking.

She scooped a little from each can and mixed the ingredients, then took the plate with her culinary creation to the table and set it down next to the book she'd been reading for the past couple of hours.

It wasn't that she found the history of jet fighter planes all that fascinating, but she was going out of her mind with boredom. And unfortunately, airplanes were the subject of each and every one of the small collection of books gathering dust over the fireplace mantel.

She'd already finished the one about the invention of modern flying machines, which had been kind of interesting, but the rest of the modest selection was mostly about famous jet fighter battles that were just too sad to read about, so she was stuck with the one in front of her.

Shoving a forkful of the mix into her mouth, she distracted herself from the bland stuff by trying to picture the cabin's owner. It was a guy, that was for certain, a bachelor or a widower, or someone that treated the cabin as his private man cave because the place was completely devoid of a woman's touch.

On the other hand, a man wouldn't have installed a claw-foot tub in the bathroom for himself. So he either had bought the cabin from a couple or had a woman and lost her... a long time ago. A widower then. Probably a veteran, maybe a survivalist...

As far as utilities, the cabin was self-sufficient, and if the guy were a hunter, he could choose to live up here indefinitely...

Oh, Fates. She hoped that wasn't what Dalhu had in mind when he brought her here.

Talk about cabin fever.

She'd rather take her chances with the bears and the coyotes and whatever else was lurking outside than stay cooped up in here and go slowly insane.

Forget slowly. It would take no more than one more day with nothing to do.

She had to find a way out.

If her assumptions about the guy who owned the cabin were true, then there was a good chance he had a rifle stashed somewhere around. Not that she planned to shoot Dalhu with it, though using it to clobber him over the head was an option...

She needed the rifle to make it to civilization without getting eaten on the way.

Why hadn't she thought about it sooner? With Dalhu gone for hours, she could've searched the place thoroughly at an easy pace.

Now, she might be already out of time.

It took her less than half an hour to conduct a frantic though thorough search to produce nothing more lethal than a broom.

She even knocked on the walls in the hopes of finding a hidden storage compartment. It wasn't completely out of left field. After all, the washer-dryer combo was hidden behind a panel in the bathroom. She would've never found it if not for the noise the machine was making. Which reminded her that the drying cycle was probably done a long time ago.

Whatever. First she had to finish the search before the sun set and before her kidnapper got back.

Opening the front door just a little more than a crack, she scanned the porch and the area around the cabin, even giving her sense of smell a go. Not that she'd ever sniffed for wild animals before, but she figured the smell of one predator ready to pounce shouldn't be all that different from another, and she was well acquainted with the smell of the most dangerous one—a male immortal. But if there was anything out there, it was too far away for her to smell.

Or at least she hoped so...

With a quick sprint, she dashed for the shed, then closed the door behind her and bolted it for good measure.

It was dark inside, but with the little light filtering through the cracks, she was able to see the single naked lightbulb hanging from the ceiling rafters. It took her a moment of searching for the light switch to realize that the string hanging down from the thing was the way to go about turning it on, and she pulled.

The good news, if one could call it that, was that there was enough wood stored in the shed to keep the cabin warm all winter long, and there were a couple of shovels in case they got snowed in. A few simple tools hung from pegs on the wall, and there was even an electric table saw. But the bad news was that there was no rifle.

Not ready to give up yet, she searched behind and under anyplace she could reach. When she didn't find anything useful, Amanda gave the shovels another glance. In a pinch, a shovel might prove handy... well, maybe against one predator, but certainly not a pack.

For clobbering Dalhu, though...

If she managed to knock him out for long enough, she could take the car. No need to fight off wild animals then.

But did she have the guts?

If she attacked him and failed, he might kill her despite all of his promises to the contrary. Though in truth? She was an immortal and not that easy to kill. Dalhu might get angry and go as far as inflicting some serious pain, but she'd never truly believed he would deliberately take the steps necessary to end her immortal life. One didn't sever a head or cut out a heart in a fit of anger.

At least she hoped not.

So why had she kept saying it? Because it sounded more dramatic than one hell of a beating, and besides, she'd gotten carried away, believing her own exaggerations.

Question was, where could she hide a shovel within easy reach?

Duh, under the couch, where else...

With the shovel in hand, she did the whole scan and sniff routine again before sprinting back to the cabin, then stashed the contraband under the couch...

Wait... that wouldn't work.

If Dalhu spent another night on the sofa, he might accidentally find it. And besides, it was stupid to hide the shovel where she would need to get close to Dalhu just to pull it out—and probably wake him before having a chance to do anything.

It would be better to hide it under the bed. Where she slept...

But wait... that wouldn't work either.

Damn.

With the new bedsheets she'd had him buy, he might offer to help her make the bed and discover the shovel hidden under it.

Oh, well, there was no other place that made sense. She had to chance it.

CHAPTER 14: KRI

"Come on, Michael, stop torturing yourself and take the meds." Why were guys so stupid? There was no reason for him to suffer through the pain of growing fangs and venom glands. Not when Dr. Bridget offered to prescribe him perfectly safe painkillers and knock him out. At least until the worst part was over.

Thank the merciful Fates, though, that this was the extent of Michael's ordeal. Syssi had almost died going through hers.

Kian must've been to hell and back watching the woman he loved fighting for her life. Poor guy. And instead of celebrating Syssi's successful transition, he was heading out on a rescue mission to bring Amanda back.

Damn, I would've liked to be on that team... Not

that Kian would've ever agreed to take a female Guardian on a mission like that. He was progressive, but not that progressive. And anyway, someone had to take care of Michael.

"No," Michael mumbled through the ice chips he'd stuffed in his mouth to numb the pain. "Ice is hepin…"

Poor baby, he couldn't even move his tongue to make the L sound. Or the G. But whose fault was that? Maybe his mentor could talk some sense into that mulish head of his. She turned to Yamanu, who'd been grinning since this whole argument had started. "Talk to him. Maybe the stubborn ass will listen to you."

"He is a big boy." Yamanu shrugged. "There were no meds when I was a boy, and I lived through it. He can tough it out if he wants to."

Kri threw her hands in the air. "Argh, you men are all idiots."

Yamanu patted her shoulder. "Let the boy be a man, Kri, and witness his own transition. Would you like to be knocked out during the most transformative event of your life? Like maybe when you become a mother?"

"You can bet your ass, I would. I'm not as dumb as some of those women who want a *natural* birthing experience. If I ever deliver a baby, I want to have all the painkillers I can get. There is no glory in unnecessary suffering." Glaring at Yamanu, she crossed her arms over her chest.

Yamanu pushed away from the wall he'd been leaning against and gave Michael a pitying glance. "Well, boy, I did my best. You're on your own. See ya later." He waved and left Bridget's recovery room.

Kri sighed and sat down on the bed next to Michael. "I just can't stand seeing you in so much pain."

Michael reached for her hand and gave it a squeeze.

"How about you at least take the codeine, it's not going to knock you out cold, just take the edge off."

Michael closed his eyes for a moment, then nodded.

"Hallelujah! I'm going to get Bridget. Don't go anywhere!" She kissed his forehead, careful to stay away from his cheeks, then hurried out to search for the doctor.

Kri found Bridget in her office, busy typing furiously on her keyboard. "Dr. Bridget, I finally managed to persuade Michael to take the codeine. Could you give it to him? Like right now? I can't stand another minute of seeing him like that."

"Sure, give me a moment. I'll be right there."

"Thank you."

My poor, proud baby, Kri thought on her way back to Michael's room—the small recovery room in Bridget's clinic he'd been staying in since he'd begun his transition.

Which brought to mind the question of Michael's future accommodations. Now that he'd become an immortal there was no reason to keep holding him in the *Guest Suite*—as they called the fancy prison cell where Michael had been spending his time until now. Their secret was now his secret as well.

He should move in with me. I need to take care of him.

Not that she had any plans of letting him go once he got better. After his transition, Michael had become a most valuable asset—the first and, for now, only male immortal not from the same matrilineal descent as the rest of her clan, and she had no intention of allowing some other clan female to steal him away from her.

Andrew, Syssi's brother, was another potential candidate, but he was older. And as they had discovered with Syssi, the older the Dormant, the harder the transition went. He might decide not to risk it. And anyway, she liked Michael. The only problem? He was so damn young. But she was in no rush. She could wait for him to mature.

Best thing to do was to stake her claim, and the sooner, the better. She needed to talk to the chief Guardian and ask his permission to move Michael to her apartment. On second thought, she should also ask Onegus for some leave of absence to take care of her guy.

First, though, she needed to make some quick redecorations before she brought Michael to her place. It was just too girly. Living alone, and not in the habit of inviting anyone over, she didn't care if her place looked like the inside of a candy store. There was pink everywhere—pink walls, a pink coverlet on her queen-sized bed, and even pink cushions on the periwinkle sofa.

But the pink, though, wasn't as embarrassing as the posters.

Hunky actors and male models were her preferred wall ornaments. And she had quite a few.

She would die of embarrassment if anyone ever saw the inside of her apartment. She was supposed to be this tough cookie, and she was, on the outside. On the inside, she liked to be a girl, and not any girl, a girly-girl.

Michael was in for one heck of a surprise.

CHAPTER 15: DALHU

While Dalhu chilled in the coffee shop across from the department store, the forty-something nothing-special he'd charmed the pants off was doing all the legwork of finding and buying the female-specific items on Amanda's list with the money he'd given her.

So, if Amanda hoped that a man like him shopping for bras and thongs and lotions would be too conspicuous to forget, Dalhu had managed to outsmart her.

Uneducated doesn't mean stupid, Professor...

The woman he'd chosen for the task had been more than happy to help poor, helpless him with the list of items his *little sister,* who was moving back home after graduating college, had asked him to buy for her.

When the woman came back, shopping bags galore, he thanked her, kissed her cheek, and promised to call.

Feeling a little guilty, he offered to pay her for her efforts, but she refused to accept the money...

Just as he'd known she would.

Her loss. He wouldn't be delivering the kind of payment he'd hinted on...

Next stop was the supermarket, where he did nothing more clandestine than slouching and drooping his shoulders to look smaller.

So all in all, he did well.

But it had taken him three hours to reach the nearest mall that had one of the department stores Amanda had listed, and about an hour and a half to complete all of the purchases. He had three more hours of driving to do.

It was getting dark by the time he drove up the steep incline of the private, unpaved road that lead up to the cabin.

Dalhu couldn't help the sense of excited anticipation as he imagined Amanda's happy welcome, especially upon discovering the gourmet cheeses he'd bought for her, not to mention the wine the lady at the cheese counter had suggested would accompany them nicely.

He'd bought four bottles. Just in case.

Except, as much as Amanda hated those pink sweats, she might go for the clothes first.

Hopefully, his personal shopper had done a good job with those. After all, he'd chosen her not for her looks, but for how well she'd been dressed.

At first, he'd intended to find a woman that looked wealthy—less chance of her running off with his money. But when his eyes had landed on, what was her name, Judy? he'd known she was exactly what he was looking for. In addition to her expensive-looking clothes, she was tall and slim and had Amanda's coloring. Though, that was where the resemblance ended. Where Amanda was a vision of beauty, poor Judy was more of a Plain Jane.

Telling her that she looked a lot like his *sister* had actually been the pickup line he'd used. And when he'd added that he liked what she was wearing and it was exactly the kind of stuff his sister would love, she had been his. Even before he'd told her to feel free to add to the list.

He hadn't bothered to check what was in the bags. Except one. He just couldn't help himself from going through the pink one from that lingerie store, Victoria's Closet, or something like that. Holding those tiny panties had given him a raging hard-on, especially the little white thong with a bow at the back. Picturing Amanda wearing it, with nothing else on, was the stuff of dreams. He imagined, in slow motion, unraveling that little knot and letting the tiny scrap of fabric flutter down to the floor…

Damn. He had no words.

Not that the woman wasn't amazing with whatever she had on—

Yeah…

Tonight was the night. Amanda would be grateful for all the nice things he'd bought her and reward him with at least a kiss. Though hopefully, he'd take that kiss and turn it into more.

As he crested the hill and the Honda's head-lights swept over the dark cabin, his eyes immediately went up to the two exposed windows under the gabled roof. They kind of looked like the eyes of a crossed-eyed giant—with the brick chimney being his nose and the slanting roof-gable on each side its brows.

The cabin had only a few light fixtures, and the light coming from those windows was dim. But with nothing else for miles around, even this was a dead giveaway.

Right. There wasn't much he could do about it.

Parking parallel to the porch, he cut the engine, popped the trunk, and shoved the keys into his pocket—all along watching the front door and hoping Amanda would throw it open and come running to greet him...

Or not...

Yeah. Whatever. He'd told her not to open the door... she was just obeying his orders...

Right, in your dreams...

"Amanda, open up!" he gave a holler as he climbed the stairs with a bunch of shopping bags in each hand, then stood by the door, waiting...

Maybe she was in the bathroom...

Or maybe she wasn't there...

As panic fought for dominance with anger, Dalhu was about to kick open the door when she finally deigned to let him in.

"What took you so long?" she accused and sauntered back to the couch, then picked up some damn book she'd been apparently reading.

Jet fighters?

"The nearest mall is three hours away, and the stuff on your list wasn't exactly something I could find at a 7-Eleven," he bit out as he dropped the bags on the floor and went for another round.

Amanda didn't offer to help or begin putting things away, and she showed no sign of interest in what he'd bought either.

Of all the ungrateful, spoiled... princesses...

He was tempted to use a less flattering word, but even inside his own head, he refused to refer to her in a derogatory way. Their relationship would be built on mutual respect—starting with his choice of language.

"Thanks for all your help," he said sarcastically.

"You're welcome," she gritted without lifting her head.

"What's your problem?"

"You have to ask? Really?"

She had a point.

It wasn't like they were a couple on their honeymoon or anything. He'd kidnapped her and was holding her prisoner in an isolated cabin. But that was old news, and she'd been in a much better mood before he'd left. What the hell had gotten into her in his absence?

Well, glancing at the book in her hands, he had to admit that she must've been damn bored during the long hours he'd been gone to be desperate enough to read about the history of jet-fighters.

With that in mind, he switched gears. "I brought brie, and camembert, and gorgonzola, and goat cheese..." he singsonged, watching her expression change as he kept taking one fancy cheese after another out of the bag and putting them in the refrigerator.

Amanda pretended to be absorbed in the book, but she was practically salivating and trying to swallow without him noticing her do so.

"You don't have to wait until I put everything away, you could come and take a bite right now. I know you want it... come and get it..." he taunted, holding a wedge of Havarti cheese and unwrapping the top.

"Oh, damn." Amanda dropped the book on the coffee table and got up. "I have no willpower. None whatsoever..." she lamented as she got closer to the cheese, her eyes focused on the thing like a hungry cat on a mouse.

But as soon as she reached for it, he lifted his arm up and caught her around the waist with the other, bringing her close for a kiss.

Taken by surprise, she didn't have time to erect her defenses, giving in to the sensation for a moment. Only for a moment, though, and then he was shoved away and pinned with the blue stare of a hungry predator. A hissing, growling, angry jungle cat that was about to scratch his eyes out if he dared taunt her even a moment longer.

"Here you are, sweetheart. It's all yours." He quickly gave her the wedge.

With another hiss, she grabbed it, pivoted on her heel, and went back to sit on the couch with her prize. She peeled away the wrap, took a big bite, and began chewing.

The expression of bliss on her face was priceless.

"Aren't you curious to see all the nice things I've got for you? I know you don't want to spend another minute wearing those sweats…"

Her eyes darted to the Macy's bags piled next to the stairs, and he knew she was fighting the urge to go and check them out.

Slowly but surely he was chipping away at her defenses.

"Well?" He arched a brow.

"Stuff from Macy's is nothing to get excited about," she finally said over a mouthful of cheese.

Maybe so, but still, he knew she was dying to dive into those bags. "As you wish… I also brought some DVDs so we could watch a movie tonight," he threw over his shoulder as he pulled a bunch of thin cases from a supermarket bag.

"And how do you propose we watch them, Sherlock? There is no TV."

"On my laptop."

That shut her up. But only momentarily.

"That's right, I forgot you had one. Not that it crossed your mind that I might have used it to entertain myself while you were gone for most of the day."

"To do what? There is no Internet here. And if there was, you think I'd be stupid enough to let you use it?"

CHAPTER 16: AMANDA

*A*manda shrugged and took another bite of the cheese.

Damn, it was hard to keep all of that anger going on. Why did Dalhu have to be so amiable all of the sudden?

Where was all that rage he had simmering just below the surface?

Did his new pleasant disposition have anything to do with him getting lucky with some chippy at the mall?

Well, that thought seemed to do the job—getting her good and angry as she imagined him pleasuring some slut with that amazing body of his...

Never mind that it proved that she was completely nuts...

Whatever, it didn't matter what caused it as long as it worked. She needed to keep up the anger for its pungent aroma to mask the scents of her anxiety and guilt. If Dalhu got a whiff of those, he might suspect something was up... as in up the stairs and under the bed...

Yep. She had lost it. Why the hell was she getting a knot in her gut every time she thought about that shovel she'd stashed upstairs?

Well, she wasn't a murderous bitch, that's why.

Not that a shovel to the head would kill Dalhu, but still, imagining his handsome face broken and bloody...

Oh, Fates, there is no way I could do it... no way!

"What's the matter?" Dalhu shot her a worried glance.

Great, now she'd given herself away.

"Nothing, I'm just antsy." She glared at him, trying to get herself angry again by imagining some other female's hands on him... unbuttoning his designer shirt, parting it to reveal his powerful chest... the tanned skin contrasting enticingly with the white fabric...

Shit. This was so not what she was going for...

"I can help with that." Dalhu's voice dropped to a growl as he breathed in, getting a lungful of the pheromones she'd just cast his way.

"No, you stay where you are… don't get any closer. I want none of that." Amanda shooed him away as he moved toward her.

"I beg to differ." Dalhu took another step, but then the panic in her eyes gave him pause, and he stopped, wiping a shaky hand over his mouth. "It's okay. I get it. Your body wants me, but your mind is still fighting it. I can wait. If what you've told me about immortal females is true, then you won't be able to hold off for much longer anyway." Dalhu swung around and began organizing the food supplies with deadly deliberation.

Unfortunately, he was right. And that was exactly why she needed to implement her plan.

Tonight.

Dalhu turned to look at her and frowned. "Why don't you take the stuff I bought you upstairs, relax with a nice bubble bath, and change into something pretty? I'm sure it would make you feel better. And by the time you're done, I'll have dinner ready."

Who was that man, and what had he done with Dalhu? Amanda shook her head in disbelief as she took a last bite of the cheese and got up. Leaving what was left of the wedge on the dining table, she grabbed as many shopping bags as she could carry and took them upstairs.

Instead of the misogynistic brute that she could easily hate, Dalhu was proving—against all odds—to be patient, respectful, and accommodating. If anyone had told her a Doomer was capable of this, she would've laughed in their faces and called them all kinds of stupid.

As she started the water for the tub, she glanced at the counter, making sure that there were a couple of fresh towels on hand.

Check her out, she was learning to be like a regular person. Yay!

And on that note, she even emptied the dryer, which had finished its cycle hours ago, and dumped the clothes on the bed. Her blouse had shrunk to something that wouldn't fit a ten-year-old, and although her pants looked fine, they were in desperate need of ironing...

She wondered if Dalhu knew how to do that.

Amanda wasn't sure she could manage even the folding. But that would wait for later. By now the tub was probably full.

Taking off the sweats, she debated between shoving them in the washing machine and dumping them in the trash, but in an uncharacteristic stroke of practicality, she decided on the machine. Who knew what Dalhu had in those bags, she thought as she slowly lowered her body into the water.

So what was his story? Was it all a very convincing act? But to what end? If he wanted to have sex with her, he could've done it already. And although she might've resisted initially, they both knew she would've quickly succumbed to her own need.

And besides, Dalhu didn't strike her as such a good actor.

But then, how the hell this walking-bomb-waiting-to-explode had managed to withstand her obnoxious act was baffling. And it wasn't as if this was all a show of admirable control either. She'd sensed only a mild surge of annoyance and disappointment when she hadn't greeted him with the excitement he'd been obviously hoping for, and then the familiar scent of determination she was starting to associate with him had quickly replaced even that.

Such a sexy combination.

A guy that was a tower of strength, physically and otherwise, and at the same time committed to making her happy in any way he could.

Except for letting her go, that is.

Shit. If he weren't a Doomer, he would've been the perfect male for her. How many guys out there would've tolerated her penchant for drama, the fact that she was a spoiled princess and was used to getting her way—always, and had a runaway mouth with no brakes.

Not to mention a history of partners as long as the list of animators in a Pixar movie.

Though be that as it may, it didn't mean she was willing to go along with his crazy plan. Staying with Dalhu meant never seeing her family again, and even if that weren't a line she drew in the sand, which of course it was, she couldn't spend her long life just as someone's mate and nothing more. She loved her job—the research, the teaching, the daily contact with minds that were hungry for knowledge. And other things…

None of that would be possible on the run.

Unfortunately, for Dalhu to keep his head attached to his shoulders, he had to keep running and hiding. If he were ever caught by his people, they would execute him for desertion, and she had no doubt Kian would tear him limb from limb for abducting her.

Her brother's deep-seated hatred for Doomers was well known.

Not that she could blame him when she felt the same.

Well, except for Dalhu.

With a sad sigh, Amanda reached for the soap.

Maybe she should have sex with the poor guy as a way to atone for later bashing his head in with a shovel as he slept. And maybe she could even leave him a note, explaining why she had to do it.

In the end, he would understand it was for the best... after healing from the injury, that is... and after reading her note.

With her gone, he would have no trouble disappearing somewhere where there was no chance of him accidentally bumping into his people. And she wasn't planning on telling Kian where she left Dalhu either, ensuring he was safe from her brother's wrath as well.

Finishing her bath in a hurry, she got out and wrapped herself in a towel, then tiptoed into the bedroom and lifted one of the paper bags.

Back in the bathroom, she tore off a good sized piece, then dropped her towel on the floor and pushed it with her foot, wedging it against the door to keep the thing closed.

Naked, she sat on the toilet to write the note. Her first attempt and the second got flushed down the drain. The third one she wrote standing up with the piece of paper lying flat against the hard surface of the counter so it would come out legible this time.

Dear Dalhu,

If you're reading this note, then my plan worked and I'm back home with my family.

Please forgive me for what I've done, and know that I'll always remember you fondly, regardless of how it all started and how it had to end.

You were nothing but kind and respectful, and it was with heavy heart that I've devised this plan to hurt you. But if you think it through, rationally, you'll realize that I did us both a service. Your plans for us, though sweet and romantic, were unrealistic.

I cannot live on the run and abandon my family and my work to be with you. I could never be happy with just being your mate, even if there were no ancient feud and hatred between our people.

You'll be safer without me and could start a new life somewhere far removed from the conflict.

Having to always look behind your back, waiting to be caught, is no way to live.

I'm not going to tell anyone about this cabin, so you have nothing to fear from my side. I'm going to invent a story of getting lost and confused and take them on a wild goose hunt, giving you the time you need to heal and disappear.

Stay safe and live your life.

Wishing you the best of luck,

Amanda.

After reading it over, she folded the note several times and placed it under the pack of band-aids in the first aid kit.

This way, when Dalhu regained consciousness and went for the kit to treat his injuries, he'd find it.

Wasn't she a clever girl?

CHAPTER 17: DALHU

*A*manda came down in a pair of skin-tight jeans, a fitted, long-sleeved black T-shirt, and no bra, her beautiful breasts bouncing enticingly with each step she took. They weren't large, but like the rest of her, they were perfectly shaped —firm and yet soft, the hard little tips at their tops absolutely mouthwatering.

Damn. Dalhu swallowed hard. The woman was fine.

She took a seat next to the table he'd set up for their dinner and flashed him that gorgeous smile of hers.

"Thank you, Dalhu."

It seemed his efforts were well worth it.

"You're welcome," he said without sarcasm.

To see her smile at him with genuine affection

in her eyes, he was willing to do much more than just put the groceries away and set a table.

What a shame there were no more dragons for him to slay or evil sorcerers to outsmart, and as it was, he was one of the not so imaginary bad guys.

Was being the imperative word.

But yeah…

Sitting across from Amanda, he watched with satisfaction as she piled her plate with chunks of assorted cheeses, crackers and some grapes, and then got to work.

A bunch of stinky cheeses wasn't what he would call a great meal—a juicy steak with some fries on the side would hit the spot for him—but for Amanda he was willing to turn off his sense of smell and even try to enjoy them.

"Aren't you going to eat?" Amanda waved her fork at his empty plate.

Dalhu reached for the bottle of wine. "I'm just taking a moment to watch you. I don't want to miss the expression of bliss on your face with each new bite you take." He pulled out the cork and filled two goblets to the rim.

"Cheers." He waited for her to lift hers and clink glasses with him.

"Not bad." She licked her lips, which sent a zing straight to his groin.

They ate in silence, with Amanda hungrily devouring everything on her plate and then going for seconds, and him mostly watching.

"Pour me another one, would you?" She raised her empty goblet.

"My pleasure." He filled it to the brim.

The woman had a healthy appetite and an impressive capacity for alcohol, drinking one-for-one with him. By the time the meal was over, they had emptied two bottles of wine.

"I'm stuffed." Amanda leaned back in her chair and rubbed her flat belly.

Oh man... in this position her breasts were clearly outlined, pushing against the fabric of her shirt, and as she let her head loll back, the pale expanse of her neck had his venom glands swell and his fangs drop down to his mouth.

Dalhu swallowed hard, his chest constricting from lack of oxygen as he forced his breathing to sound normal. Otherwise, it would've come out harsh and loud like a locomotive. "Time for a movie?" He got up and began to clear the table.

From the corner of his eye, he saw Amanda lift her arms over her head, which had her shirt stretch farther across her breasts and ride up to reveal the soft expanse of her middle.

She pushed away from the table and picked up their empty plates. "Let me help."

Stifling a groan, he took the things out of her hands. "No need, sweetheart. You go and sit on the couch. Pick a movie you'd like to watch while I finish here."

"Well, if you insist..." she slurred lazily, apparently having no problem following instructions when it suited her.

A few moments later he joined her on the couch. "So, what will it be?" He wrapped an arm around her shoulders. When she didn't protest, he was pleasantly surprised.

Maybe she didn't notice...

"I'm deliberating between *The Princess Bride* and *The Avengers*. Have you seen either of them?" She lifted the two movies for him to examine the covers.

"I've seen *The Avengers*, great movie, but not the other one. I picked it thinking a princess like you would like it..."

"I do like it. The guy only said *'as you wish'* to the girl. What's not to like?"

"*Princess Bride* it is, unless you'd rather watch *The Avengers*. I don't mind watching it again."

"No, I think you should watch the princess one. You could learn a thing or two." She smirked.

Dalhu freed the disk from the elaborate wrapping and popped it into his laptop's disk drive.

"I'm surprised you got to watch movies. I thought all *corrupt* Western media was forbidden."

"We were advised to watch with caution, and only action flicks. After all, how do you think I got to sound like I was born and raised in the US when, in fact, it's my first time here? Learning to speak like a native was the perfect excuse to watch shitloads of movies."

"Really? This is your first time here?" Amanda regarded him with what he hoped was newfound appreciation. "I must admit this is really impressive. I would've never guessed."

"Thank you." Dalhu felt like he'd just grown another inch or two.

"So tell me, did you learn to speak English so well just from watching movies? Or does the Brotherhood provide language courses?"

"No, not really." He chuckled. "The only education they provide are basic reading and writing skills, and even this is a recent development. They started it less than a hundred years ago, and only for the commanders. It took another twenty years until they realized that literacy was an essential skill in modern times, even for the rank and file. For foreign languages, they supply us with stuff like the Rosetta Stone courses, and we teach ourselves."

"Well, it's probably good enough. Our kind is uniquely talented in that department. Absorbing a new language is so easy for me, it takes me a couple of weeks at most of hanging with the locals in a new country to speak like a native, but I usually don't bother with the reading and writing. Not unless I have a good reason to." She smiled apologetically as if she was embarrassed to admit it.

Dalhu dipped his head to hide his grimace. What would Amanda think of him if she knew how limited his education was? That he had been illiterate for most of his life?

He wasn't going to tell her, and if she asked, he wouldn't flat out lie, but he wouldn't give her a straight answer either. She already had a pretty low opinion of him, and the last thing he needed was to dump this boulder on the negative side of the scale.

Luckily, she dropped the subject.

Things got even better as the movie started, and Amanda got comfortable, leaning back into his arm and completely stunning him by resting her head on his shoulder.

It was heaven to hold her close, her body soft

and relaxed in his embrace. But it was hell to fight the urge to take this thing further.

There was no way she didn't know what she was doing to him. And not just because she was an immortal like him, who most likely could scent his lust, but because he couldn't control his breathing anymore, not without choking, and his breaths were coming in and going out, chuffing like a fucking locomotive. The cause would've been obvious to anyone.

Yeah, she was definitely aware.

She didn't remain unaffected, though. It seemed that as his breathing got heavier, hers was getting shallower, and he could've sworn her breasts were swelling, or maybe it was just the effect of her nipples getting harder and protruding farther.

He wasn't paying attention to the movie, and although Amanda had her eyes on the small laptop screen, pretending to watch, he suspected she paid it as much attention as he did.

The Princess Bride had just become his favorite movie of all times…

With gentle fingers, Dalhu took hold of Amanda's chin and tilted her head—so she was staring up at his eyes as he dipped down and kissed her lips, slowly.

Amanda didn't pull away.

She moaned, her chest heaving with pent-up desire as she parted her lips and invited him to deepen the kiss.

He brought them closer, kissing her harder, and still she didn't resist. Getting bolder, he reached under her T-shirt and rested his palm on the soft skin of her belly.

With a groan, Amanda covered his hand with her palm. But instead of pushing it away as he'd expected her to, she pushed it up to her breast—a shudder running through her upon contact.

Holy Mortdh, he didn't need a written invitation to get that he was just given the green light.

Gently, he lowered her down to the couch and pushed her T-shirt up and over her beautiful breasts, then pulled back to stare at the magnificent beauty he'd just unveiled.

He wanted to dive in and suckle her, to take turns with each puckered nipple until he got his fill...

Which could take a while...

Except, to pleasure her properly, he needed to take it slow and learn to play Amanda's body like one would learn to play a fine instrument, paying close attention to what she liked and what she did not. And that required two things he was in short supply of.

Patience and restraint.

Reaching to cup her breasts, he had a feeling that his hands shook a little, though if they did, it was barely perceptible. He groaned with pleasure. Perfect; the hard tips tickling the inside of his palms, and just the right size to fill his cupped hands but not overflow them.

Fighting the urge to descend on her with his lips and his tongue, he started slowly circling her turgid peaks with his thumbs, making contact only with the areola, teasing her, expecting her to urge him to do more. But besides arching her spine to push her breasts into his hands, she did nothing to protest his little teasing.

For some reason, Amanda was holding back.

Which troubled him.

By now he had a pretty good idea of the kind of woman she was, and meek wasn't it.

Dalhu had no problem with taking the lead, or with dominating the hell out of her, but only if this was what turned her on, and not because she was frightened.

Letting his senses probe deeper, he detected a hint of trepidation. But that was to be expected, it was no more than the thrill of a new partner, and nothing that would explain her timid response.

"We don't have to do this..." he murmured, even though it would kill him to stop.

"It's my first time... with an immortal..." She smiled a lopsided smile.

Aha... so that's her game...

No problem, he could play along...

"It's my first time as well... with one untried, that is... but you have nothing to fear, my sweet. I'll go slow and gentle and make sure it's good for you." He moved his thumbs back and forth across her hard tips before dipping his head and pulling one between his lips.

She bucked under him, but not to throw him off...

"Do you like this?" he breathed over her wet nipple.

"Oh, Fates, yeeees..." she mewled.

He suckled her other nipple, swirling his tongue around the tip and tugging gently with his fingers on its twin.

Dalhu took his time, alternating between using his fingers and his mouth, savoring each one of Amanda's throaty moans. When he sensed she'd had enough, he cupped her wet breasts and took her mouth in a hard kiss. She opened for him, drawing his tongue into her mouth.

When he came up for air, she grasped the hem of her T-shirt, yanked it over her head, and tossed it behind her.

Timid no more, she shifted up and reached for the buttons of his shirt, kissing him while she was at it, slipping her tongue between his lips and sweeping it against his.

Dalhu leaned back and Amanda moved to straddle him, her core hot over his rock-hard shaft even through the barrier of fabrics between them. Getting busy with the buttons, she rocked against him, kissing every little bit of skin she was exposing. He kept stroking her back and her waist and the sides of her bare breasts, running his ragged palms all over that soft, smooth skin.

When she parted the two halves, he helped her peel the shirt off his shoulders. And as she tugged on it, he leaned forward so she could pull it free. Giving the shirt a little spin over her head, Amanda sent the thing flying in the same direction her T-shirt went.

Admiring his bare chest, she looked like a triumphant goddess, as if he belonged to her—was hers to do with as she pleased.

Yes he was, and he had absolutely no problem

with this.

After a moment, she hissed and latched on to his neck, licking, kissing, nibbling. And as she kept rocking and undulating her hips over his groin, her wet nipples rubbed against his chest.

The good news was that Amanda seemed to have forgotten that she wanted to play the shy virgin. The bad news was that with what she was doing, he wasn't going to last. With his fangs already down in his mouth, and precum wetting his jeans, he was either going to rip her pants off and plunge right in or explode in his pants.

Neither was acceptable.

Wrapping an arm tightly around her upper body and clamping a palm over her butt, he stilled her gyrations. "You have to stop... Unless you're ready to get straight down to business," he part hissed, part slurred through his fangs.

Amanda pulled back a little, gasping at the sight of him. "Can I touch them?" She kept her eyes on his fangs as she brought her pointer finger to hover a fraction of an inch away from the sharp tip.

"Yeah..." he breathed, his abdominals contracting in excited anticipation of her touch.

Very gently, she ran her finger all the way from his swollen gum down to the tip and pressed lightly, just enough for it to pierce her skin and draw a tiny drop of blood.

They both moaned when he swirled his tongue around her injured digit, the taste of her blood exploding over his senses as he healed the small nick.

"Fuck, Amanda..." His hips surged involuntarily, pressing his hard length up to her center. "This isn't helping..."

"I'm sorry," she whispered, wrapping her arms around him. With her slim palm holding on to his nape, she buried her nose in the crook of his neck. "I wanted to take it slow and savor this experience..." she mumbled against his skin. "Fates, I'm such a slut..." She sighed.

"Please don't..." Dalhu smoothed his palm over her bare back.

With the reminder of her sordid past, his arousal cooled as if a bucket of ice was dropped on the thing. At the same time, however, he hated that she felt this way. He wanted their first time to be all about her, her pleasure. Any guilt or shame, or whatever other negative feelings she might have, were unwelcome between them.

"No, it's true. With mortals, I take whatever I want, how I want it. I'm running the show... I use them." She chuckled, her exhale tickling his skin.

"My boy toys..." she kept talking into his neck, holding on tight as if afraid he would push her away. "I wanted... heck... I'm not sure what I wanted... I wanted it to be different with you."

Something wet and warm slid down his neck —a tear.

"Oh, hell, Amanda, that's nothing to cry about. I know exactly what it's like, and all of those that came before, for you as well as for me, don't count. They were an upgraded version of a toy to masturbate with—a semi-decent substitute, but a substitute nonetheless. Did you ever have feelings for any of them? Or use them more than once or twice?"

She shook her head, rubbing her wet nose on his skin in the process. Not that he gave a fuck if she got some snot on him...

"You see? I'm right." Dalhu cupped her cheek and gently pushed her face up from her hiding place so she had to look into his eyes. "For real? This is like the first time for both of us, with the added advantage of actually knowing what the fuck we're doing. Right?"

"I guess... we sure do know how to fuck..." Amanda smiled her teasing smile, the spark of mischief once again glinting in her big, blue eyes.

Thank fuck.

CHAPTER 18: SYSSI

*A*s the blinking lights of the helicopter vanished in the distance, Syssi closed her eyes and let the tears flow freely. It had been such a struggle to keep the waterworks at bay for Kian and Andrew's sake. Not that she'd done such an admirable job of it. But now, standing alone on the roof of Kian's high-rise, in the middle of the night, there was no more need for pretense.

No one could see her.

Except, the tears weren't enough, she still felt like choking.

It was all too much, and the stress had finally gotten the better of her.

Or was it the transition?

According to Dr. Bridget, everything in Syssi's body was supposedly in flux, and that probably included her hormones. But whether she was being hormonal or not, she knew of only one way to get some small measure of relief, and it was to let it all go, break down completely and sob her heart out.

She did, noisily, hiccups and runny nose and all, using the bottom of her T-shirt to wipe her nose and the fountains of tears from her eyes. It was soaked.

Ugh, gross.

Ah, what the heck, the thing is beyond salvage anyway. She blew her nose on one side of the shirt and gave her face a good wipe down with the other. She then took a deep, shaky breath, and another.

Snap out of it, everything is going to be fine. Her brother and the two friends he'd brought on the mission were professionals—experts in hostage retrieval, and Kian's bodyguards, Brundar and Anandur, were obviously well-trained.

But what about Kian?

She wasn't sure about his fighting skills, but he'd surely carried that wicked-looking sword like it was an extension of his body, like it was nothing new to him. And he certainly was old enough to have lived at a time when men had waged war with swords.

She wondered if he'd fought in actual battles or just knew how to wield a sword for self-defense, or maybe for sport—fencing. But even as she thought it, deep down she knew the truth.

Don't be naive. Of course, he'd fought... he had to...

Kian had the bearing of a general, and it wasn't because he was Regent over the American part of his clan. Politicians, even presidents of countries, didn't have this particular aura around them—not unless they came from a military background.

But it was a good thing, right? As an experienced fighter, Kian was less likely to get injured.

Oh, God, what if...

Stop it. No one is going to get hurt. Well, except for that Doomer. Syssi shivered as she imagined what Kian would do to that guy.

As much as she loved him, there was still a lot she didn't know about Kian, and she suspected that there was a whole other side to him she had only caught glimpses of.

His beast, as he called it. As if there was some creature or separate entity living inside of him that was wild and untamable. Right. A convenient way to excuse lack of control. She had no doubt, though, that Kian was capable of killing. And she had the uneasy feeling that he wasn't beyond cruelty either.

Would it affect the way she felt about him if she knew that for a fact? Would she be wary of him?

Probably not.

Did she want to know?

No, not really.

Coward.

Yes, she was. War and its ugliness were, unfortunately, an integral part of life, and the strong had to do what needed to be done to defend the defenseless. While Kian had no choice but to fight against enemies that threatened his clan, killing and maybe even torturing for information, she had the luxury of hiding her head in the sand as one of the defenseless.

Still, even though she fully accepted Kian, darker side and all, she felt sorry for him. The man had selflessly sacrificed a part of his soul so others could live. Not that she would ever let him know that she did.

Kian was such a guy, so proud.

She smiled, remembering his smug expression when she'd called him Superman. Indeed.

I'm so lucky. I snagged such an incredible man... immortal...

Once he returned, victorious of course, and had a chance to catch up on his sleep, she was going to put his superhuman endurance to the test with her own new and improved body.

That's right, now that she was an immortal, Kian could really let go of his *beast* and ravage her to his heart's content. She was indestructible.

In a much better mood, Syssi got back inside the rooftop vestibule and pressed the button for the elevator. It was good that the penthouse level had one that was dedicated. She would've been mortified to encounter anyone and get caught looking like she did, with puffy red eyes, red wet nose, and a shirt covered in snot. Lucky for her, both of the penthouse occupants weren't there.

Oh, God! Lucky was such an inappropriate word. Amanda wasn't home because a dangerous Doomer held her captive, and Kian wasn't home because he was on his way to rescue his sister. The situation was as far from lucky as it could get.

Bad, bad Syssi.

And the floor wasn't completely deserted either. Annani, Kian's mother, was staying at Amanda's with her two servants. And there was Okidu, Kian's butler, and Onidu, Amanda's.

Kian had suggested that she wait for the team's return with Annani.

Not a bad idea, because she really didn't want to be alone, and Okidu wasn't exactly good company—the guy had the personality of a mannequin.

But first, a change of clean clothes was in order, and she had to do something about her blotchy face. On second thought, a quick fix wouldn't do. To look presentable enough for another audience with the goddess, Syssi would need to invest a lot more effort in sprucing up.

CHAPTER 19: ANDREW

ndrew's stomach was giving him a hard time. Nothing new there, it always did on helicopter rides—no matter how many missions he'd flown.

Was it the noise? The change in altitude?

Because it sure as hell wasn't fear.

At least not for himself.

Hell, he prayed Amanda was all right.

But he knew better than to delude himself that she'd remained unharmed. The best he could hope for was that she was still alive and that whatever damage the motherfucker had done to her would heal. Except, rape was particularly hard to recuperate from. Probably impossible. Unlike injury or even torture, the part of one's soul that got ripped out by that particularly vile act of violence could never be fully restored.

Fuck. The worst part was not knowing.

It had been easier when he hadn't known the victim. It wasn't that he hadn't felt for the other abductees or their families, but to be a professional in this type of business one had to develop an emotional barrier—a numbness. Feelings led to mistakes—mistakes with life or death conse-quences. He imagined that surgeons had to develop a similar detachment. That's why they were advised to never operate on a family member.

Unless there was no other choice—like in this case. And besides, he wasn't a family member. Not yet. He'd met Amanda only once. Except, with a woman like her, the impact had been profound.

Andrew glanced at his watch again.

He estimated another fifteen minutes to touch-down, and then about two hours of trekking through the woods for a stealth attack.

Sitting next to him, Kian looked just as grim. Now that there was no more need to front confi-dence for Syssi's sake, the poor bastard looked tortured, probably by the same kinds of thoughts that were twisting Andrew's gut.

Not counting the pilot, they had four more

guys on the rescue team, which should be more than enough if Kian was right in his assessment that Amanda was being held by a single guy.

But if Kian was wrong, they were fucked.

Jake and Rodney, the guys Andrew had brought on the mission, were buddies from his old unit and he knew he could count on their professionalism. But although Kian's guys, Brundar and his redheaded brother, gave off a vibe of experienced soldiers, they had no experience with hostage retrieval.

Fuck.

Between an overwrought brother and the two deadly cousins there were too many wild cards in the mix, but apparently he needed their special abilities.

The kidnapper wasn't the usual variety of scumbag.

He was a near-immortal.

Like them.

Andrew still had trouble wrapping his head around the immortal thing. Not that he doubted what he'd been shown, but man, what a trip down the rabbit hole.

It wasn't easy to adjust to the fact that the reality he was familiar with was only part of the story, and that besides governments and economic forces there were also two factions of immortals who manipulated the show from behind the cover of shadows.

The one good and the other evil—to put it in simplistic terms.

And the kicker was that apparently he and his sister belonged to this exclusive tribe, with the caveat that unless activated, those superior genes they were lucky enough to inherit from their mother would remain dormant.

Syssi had gotten activated by the big guy sitting next to him, but her transition hadn't gone as smoothly as Kian and his people had hoped it would. It had been touch and go for a while.

Thankfully, Andrew had been spared the gut-wrenching worry by showing up on the scene after the fact.

As big and as freaky as his sister's boyfriend was, he would've killed the bastard for putting her in harm's way…

Or at least given it his best try…

As he'd been told, killing one of these immortals was next to impossible, and Andrew had neither fangs nor venom, not yet anyway, and he wasn't armed with a sword to slice off a head or cut out a heart either.

Kian, on the other hand, was well prepared and

fully equipped. Besides the deadly instruments he'd been born with, he'd brought a wicked-looking blade just for that purpose.

Gruesome, but effective.

Andrew wondered how it would feel to have deadly weapons as an integral part of his body. Was the experience different from that of an MMA fighter, or of how the knowledge affected any other guy who was deadly with his bare hands?

How would he feel after the transition?

Damn, having fangs would be so weird…

What was really surprising, though, was that he and his sister and only one other guy, Michael—a student at Amanda's university—were the first dormant carriers of those special genes that Kian's people had ever found. The rest of their clan members were all related to each other, descending from one single female and some anonymous mortal sperm donors.

The plan was, after they brought Amanda home, of course, for Andrew to go through the process as well. But he wasn't sure he was going to go for it. Not that becoming an invincible immortal didn't appeal to him, or that becoming a possible mate for Amanda wasn't as tempting as hell, but the flip side was that he might end up dead instead of immortal.

And that would really suck.

Given that Syssi, fourteen years his junior, had such a hard time transitioning, chances were good he wouldn't make it through the ordeal at all.

Good thing Kian didn't try to sugarcoat it for him, telling him the risks straight up.

Decent guy that immortal. Syssi could've done worse.

Glancing sideways at Kian, Andrew smiled a little. His future brother-in-law was one handsome motherfucker. No wonder he had Syssi wrapped around his little finger in such a short time...

True, no one was talking about a wedding yet, but they'd better, or else...

And besides, once they got hitched, there was a good chance they'd make him a little niece or a nephew, and that he wouldn't mind at all.

Not. At. All.

And if they had a boy, they could name him Jacob... after the brother he and Syssi had tragically lost.

CHAPTER 20: KIAN

ouching. Kian glanced at Andrew's tough profile as he got a whiff of the guy's fear. It must be for Amanda because Andrew didn't strike him as one who had any qualms about jumping head-on into danger.

Unfortunately, it wasn't as if Kian could assuage Andrew's worry by telling him that Annani had seen her daughter unharmed—in a vision.

He himself had trouble putting much faith in his mother's mystical remote viewing, despite her proven record.

Knowing the kinds of animals the Doomers were, it was too much of a stretch for him to suspend belief.

Fuck! It was an insult to animals to equate them with that evil...

Still, he had to believe Amanda was alive. She was, after all, too valuable to kill.

Fates, he hoped she hadn't revealed her true identity. As an immortal female, she was valuable enough, but if the fucker were to discover that he was holding Annani's daughter, the consequences would be disastrous. Currently, the Doomer's agenda seemed to be of a personal nature—grab an immortal female and keep her for himself. But Annani's daughter was a ticket to fame and glory that the fucker might be tempted to cash, and surrender her to Navuh.

The Doomers could demand anything they wanted and get it in exchange for Amanda.

No, she wasn't that stupid. Though that being said, with his sister's runaway mouth, she might've been dumb enough to goad the fucker into a murderous rage...

Which she probably had...

No, he couldn't think this way. Amanda must be alive, and whatever else the fucker had done to her, she was strong enough to survive it.

She'd heal.

The fucker, on the other hand, was a dead man. Kian was going to kill that Doomer himself. And if

Annani had a problem with that, tough. For this, he was more than willing to sacrifice his mother's approval and disregard her standing order to keep any Doomers they caught in stasis instead of offing them for good.

Unfortunately, with his venom glands swelling and his fangs pulsating within his mouth, Kian had a feeling the sword he'd brought specifically for the purpose of slicing the fucker's head off would remain unsullied in its scabbard.

Death by venom was too kind for that animal…

Tearing out the fucker's throat, though…

Fuck. He was reverting to a beast himself, wasn't he?

Kian heaved a sigh. If his sweet Syssi knew the kinds of thoughts he was harboring, she would run screaming.

Poor girl.

Instead of the romantic dinner he'd promised to take her on, she'd spent the night unconscious while her body had fought to survive the transition.

She could've died if his mother hadn't come to the rescue…

He would've never forgiven himself if she…

Yeah, better not go there.

170

Lately, it seemed that he couldn't make a move without it turning into a disaster.

His instructions to speed up the rate with which the clan had traditionally transferred information to mortals had resulted in Mark's exposure and subsequent murder by Doomers. Syssi almost dying was, of course, his fault. It had been his fangs and his venom that had facilitated her transition. Even Amanda's kidnapping was his fault. If he hadn't insisted on Syssi going shopping and taking Amanda with her, his sister would've never crossed paths with that Doomer.

The chances of the fucker bumping into her accidentally were so negligible that it almost seemed like the cursed Fates had a hand in it.

But why?

What had he or Amanda ever done to deserve such punishment?

Damn, he was losing his mind…

Fates…

Really…

Don't tempt the Fates, Kian, his mother's voice sounded in his head.

Yep, he was definitely losing it.

CHAPTER 21: AMANDA

*D*ear Fates, the man was impossible.

As those big brown eyes of his gazed at her with such tender emotion, the idea of clobbering Dalhu with a shovel made her feel like dirt.

"I could never just fuck you." Dalhu's palms were still on her cheeks as he shifted up and placed a gentle kiss on her lips. "I will worship your body with mine, make love to you the way a rare treasure like you should be made love to," he breathed.

Okay, now he made her feel lower than dirt—more like a piece of dung.

To hide her perfidy, she kissed him back, funneling all of her guilt and self-loathing into the kind of desperate passion that had her cling to him as if she would never let go.

DARK ENEMY TAKEN

Only when the lack of oxygen made her dizzy did she release his mouth and buried her face in the crook of his neck. "I would like that," she whispered against his skin.

With his powerful arms wrapped around her, Dalhu held her to him, clinging just as desperately, his chest heaving as he gulped air into his oxygen-deprived lungs.

"I want to spend hours learning your body an inch at a time." He eased up on his tight hold as he moved his palm up and down her spine.

Such a lovely sentiment. Problem was, he'd drive her absolutely crazy like that, and in no time she'd take over and drive them home...

Except, she wanted this to go Dalhu's way, for this one time they had together to be about his pleasure. A parting gift so he'd remember her as something other than the underhanded, conniving slut that she was.

"You'd better tie me up, then..." she blurted in a hurry.

"What? No...! I would never do that." Dalhu sounded horrified by the suggestion. "I only want to bring you pleasure..." He pulled back a little and dipped his head to look into her eyes. "Whatever you want, however you want it."

What a sweet man... And to think she was talking about a Doomer...

Amanda palmed his scruffy cheek. "I want to experience something new—something different with you. But patience is not one of my strong points, nor is relinquishing even a tiny bit of control to another, and I don't want to spoil it for both of us by taking over and speeding things up. All I need is a reminder, like a T-shirt or some other piece of clothing tied around my wrists. You do know that I'm strong enough to rip it apart if I want to, right?"

"You are?"

"Dalhu, darling, you keep forgetting that I'm not a mortal. And just as you're stronger and faster than a mortal male, so am I compared to human females." She ran her hands over the sculpted perfection of his chest. "Though with that magnificent body of yours, I suspect you're stronger than most immortal males as well."

"Really... so you want to tell me that you could've gotten free from those handcuffs I used on you?" Dalhu's smile was conceited.

"Like I didn't know those were reinforced... Which begs the question of why you had them in the first place..." She eyed Dalhu suspiciously.

"You said my kidnapping wasn't planned. So what gives?"

"It wasn't. And the reason behind the cuffs is no longer relevant. Let's just forget it…"

"Tell me."

"I don't want to spoil the mood."

"If you don't spill, there'll be nothing to spoil."

Amanda felt like banging her head against a wall. She was such an idiot—so damn stupid it was criminal.

Here she was in a unique position to learn the enemy's dastardly plans for her family, but instead of using her head to pump Dalhu for information, all she could think about was the kind of pumping that involved both of them getting sweaty…

Dalhu sighed, his expression turning utterly despondent. "Before I answer, I just want you to know that everything is different now. I would never hurt you by hurting your family. But before I got to know you, before I pledged my future and myself to you, I was part of an organization that expected me to deliver certain results. I won't lie to you; I wasn't some big shot, but I wasn't just a mindless cog following orders either."

Wiping a nervous hand over his mouth, Dalhu sighed again. "I came up with the idea that males of your clan could be found where mortal females went searching for hookups. I planned on apprehending such a male to learn from him the location of your center of operation."

Deflated, he dropped his arms to his sides and leaned back against the couch cushions, his head falling back. But if he expected her to get off him, he was dead wrong. Up close and personal, bare chest to bare chest, she had the kind of leverage that would keep him talking.

"Would I be right to assume that this plan is still in effect without you?"

"Yes, the men I left behind are a bunch of incompetent morons, and they'll do nothing without me, but reinforcements are coming—a large contingent this time—and they are likely to send someone higher up on the chain of command to lead them."

Oh, that was just getting better and better…

"When are they going to get here?"

Dalhu lifted his head, a spark of hope lightening the pits of darkness his eyes had become.

"I don't know exactly, but the leader with a few men could arrive as early as tomorrow night. The good news is that a contingent this large will require a few days at the least to take care of the logistics before the rest of the men could get here, and then they'll need more time to get organized.

It leaves plenty of time to warn your family to take preemptive measures."

"You would do that for me? For real?" Amanda searched Dalhu's eyes for signs of deception.

"You can write an e-mail to someone who knows you well and include something only you and that person are privy to, some anecdote or a private joke that'll convince them you sent it out of your own free will. Tomorrow, first thing in the morning, I'll drive to a Starbucks and use their free Wi-Fi to send it. I just hope you know somebody who will take it seriously and is in a position to do something about it."

"Do I know someone..." Amanda snorted, but then the red light in her addled brain flashed the stage-five alarm, and she closed her big mouth before blurting who she really was.

The way Dalhu kept calling her princess, it was easy to forget he had no clue she was Annani's daughter. And despite his professed loyalty to her, she'd be stupid to trust him with that piece of information.

After all, before pledging himself to her just thirty-something hours ago, he'd been a member of the Brotherhood for eight centuries. And he'd already proven that switching loyalties in a heartbeat wasn't a problem for him.

Finding out that he had Annani's daughter in his possession, he might come to the realization that she was more valuable to him as an asset he could surrender to Navuh in exchange for a prime position in the organization than the mate that he'd been fantasizing about.

"Who is it? Do you know a Guardian? It would be great if you do. A Guardian would be taken seriously."

"Yeah... that was exactly who I've been thinking of. I have a girlfriend on the force. We go clubbing together, a lot, so there are quite a few memories only she and I share..."

Dalhu looked stunned—his mouth gaping a little.

Oh, come on, like it was such a big revelation that she'd been clubbing.

"You guys have females on the force?" he gasped, apparently horrified not at the idea of her prowling for men at clubs, but that there were female Guardians.

Well, only one. For now...

And he didn't need to know that...

"Welcome to the twenty-first century, Dalhu," Amanda singsonged, not bothering to conceal her condescending tone.

"Are you guys out of your fucking minds? Who

was the moron that came up with that brilliant idea?" Dalhu's eyes darkened again, the irises barely distinguishable from the pupils.

What the hell got his panties in a wad? Not that she thought he was wearing any... The guy was practically seething with rage, which proved that his theory about her touch's magically calming effect was complete crap.

"I know that Doomers still live in the dark ages, but come on, Dalhu, I'm surprised that you still hold on to these kinds of bullshit ideas. Women can run countries, fly jets, and aside from growing a set, they can do pretty much whatever males can do. With today's weaponry, one can be a soldier or a policewoman without having to be physically powerful."

He regarded her as if she was missing a couple of screws. "You think this is about some misogynistic crap? Are you blind to the kind of enemy you guys are sending those females against? Do you have any idea what a female would endure if she were captured? Any fucking idea?"

The vehemence in his voice was getting to Amanda, her gut clenching in a surge of fear and worry. "What?" she whispered, although her mind was already supplying the answer.

"The worst kind of hell imaginable. She would

pray for the death that would never come. Should I say more? Or do you get the picture?"

Oh, she got the picture all right. Though knowing Kian, her brother would never risk sending Kri against Doomers. He used the girl primarily for situations that required—or were benefited by—a female taking care of things; like the handling of female clan offenders, and for other internal law enforcement matters.

That being said, though, it wasn't such a big stretch to imagine a situation in which Kri might be dragged into a fight with Doomers. Like when serving as a bodyguard for Amanda or Annani.

"I get the picture. Thank you very much. But the female Guardians perform only policing duties. No one in their right mind would send them against Doomers. We are well aware of the consequences."

"Thank heavens." Sinking back into the couch, Dalhu relaxed visibly, his body losing its rigidity. "Even before I met you, I would never, ever have surrendered a female immortal into the hands of my exalted leader. Never." From the way he'd hissed *my exalted leader,* Dalhu's opinion of Navuh was clear. "Nor to any of my brethren. In fact, I would've killed whoever needed killing to free her."

Dalhu kept surprising her at every turn. "My knight in shining armor." Amanda planted a loud kiss on his mouth.

Unless… it was one hell of an act to get her to like him…

Nah… To think that he was such an amazing actor was even more incredible than believing she was looking at the only Doomer with a conscience… a brain… and a heart.

Move aside, Wizard, and bow before Amanda—the new queen of Oz…

"You mean it? Or was it sarcasm I somehow missed…" Dalhu cocked a brow.

"No, I mean it. But you have to swear to me that you're going to send that e-mail tomorrow, first thing in the morning."

"I swear."

"Not good enough. I want you to make a binding oath."

"What do you want me to swear on? I'm sure you don't want to invoke Mortdh's name… unless you are calling on the devil, and as far as I know, you guys do not worship your matriarch that way. And anyway, it wouldn't mean anything to me."

He had a point. There was nothing the guy held sacred, nothing he believed in. Dalhu was mostly opportunistic and self-serving. Though, strangely, he was grounded in some internal moral code that against all odds, considering the attitude of the rest of his buddies, was very protective of women…

Eureka!

"Swear on your mother's memory."

His expression changed in a heartbeat. "How did you know?" he breathed.

"I listened when you told me about her, and it didn't require a degree in psychology to figure out that she meant a lot to you… I bet she still does. She is the flickering flame that kept your soul from being consumed by the darkness you were submerged in, the light that kept a tiny grain of hope alive in your heart. So yeah… I think you would never tarnish her memory by breaking an oath you took in her name."

"I think I've just fallen in love with you."

Did he just say that? Must've been only a figure of speech… Still, her heart fluttered a little. No one had ever said these words to her before.

No one.

"That's very sweet, but I still need the oath, Dalhu."

He took hold of her hand and placed it over his heart, then covered it with his. "I swear on my mother's memory, and that of my sister, that tomorrow morning I will send the e-mail you'll write to your friend, and with the exception of anything that might point to our location, I will make no changes to it."

"That's good. A very nice oath..." Amanda couldn't help but get a little teary... And it had nothing to do with being dramatic... for a change.

Dalhu's sincere vow touched her heart.

"I'm glad you approve." He lifted his finger and wiped away the tear that slid from the corner of her eye. "And I meant what I said before, about falling in love with you. You see me. The real me. The part that is hidden and protected by layers upon layers of heavy armor. The essence of me that no one aside from my mother and sister has ever gotten a glimpse of."

Lifting her hand to his lips, he kissed it, then did the same thing with the other. "Thank you."

Oh, boy, at this rate she'd be spouting the 'L' word back in no time...

Well, maybe not.

Nonetheless, there was no way in hell she was going to use that damned shovel now...

It was such a relief to forsake that abominable plan. She felt as if the darkness in her chest—that foreign evil thing that had taken residence inside her—got sucked up through the top of her head and dissipated.

Whatever, the important thing was that it was gone, and as she sagged against Dalhu and felt her muscles loosen, she became aware of the cramping in her legs.

With a sigh, she lifted her knee and shifted sideways to plop down on the couch.

Stretching like a cat, she lowered her legs over Dalhu's lap and her arms over the armrest, her naked breasts jutting as her body formed a gentle bow.

Dalhu's eyes zeroed right on target. "You still want me to tie you up?" The question was delivered with a rasp that suggested he no longer found the idea repugnant. In fact, he seemed quite eager.

In answer, Amanda crossed her wrists and wiggled her fingers.

"Go for it, big boy. I'm all yours."

CHAPTER 22: SYSSI

After a quick shower, a fresh change of clothes, and a makeup job to make an undertaker proud, Syssi was ready to face Annani.

She was wearing a pair of designer jeans and a silk blouse, one of the new fancy outfits Amanda had made her buy, or rather bought for her using Kian's credit card. The whole stack of them must've been delivered sometime during Syssi's stay in Bridget's hospital room.

God, she still couldn't believe that she'd been so close to not making it through, or that she'd really transitioned. It all seemed like a dream, or a nightmare, depending on how this night would end.

With a sigh, she knocked on Amanda's door.

A moment later, Onidu opened it. "Mistress, please, come in. The Clan Mother has been expecting you." He bowed and waved his arm in invitation, pointing her toward the open terrace doors.

Strangely, Syssi heard several voices as she neared the terrace. Was Annani entertaining someone else at a time like this?

But as she stepped outside, the source of what she'd heard turned out to be a tablet. Annani was watching a comedy, and at one point even giggled like a schoolgirl.

God, what a strange family. Two of her children were facing deadly danger, and she was watching some silly sitcom. At a time like this, any normal mother would be pulling out hairs, or biting nails, or crying...

Well, Annani isn't a normal mother.

A normal mother didn't sit in a pool of her own illumination, one that was radiating from her own body, and her giggles didn't sound like the chiming of an angel. Nor was she more ancient than most civilizations yet looked like a seventeen-year-old girl.

Oh, boy, Annani was going to take some getting used to.

Lifting her head away from the screen, the goddess smiled. "Hello, my dear, come, join me."

"Thank you," Syssi said as she took a seat across

from Annani.

"No, no, come and sit here beside me." Annani patted the chair next to her.

Reluctantly, Syssi did as she was told. It was still quite unnerving to get so close to all that freakish light.

Annani reached for Syssi's hand and clasped it. "Do not worry, Syssi, everything is going to be all right." She sounded confident.

"How can you be so sure?" Syssi's voice trembled a little.

"Because I know that boy is not going to hurt Amanda."

That boy? Was she calling that evil Doomer a boy? What was wrong with this woman, goddess, whatever?

Annani patted Syssi's hand. "Do not look so incredulous. When I saw Amanda, she did not look like a woman afraid for her life or even her safety. She had this smug smile on her face that could only mean she has that boy wrapped around her little finger like she does every other male."

"What do you mean, you saw her?"

"Remote viewing, of course," Annani said as if it should've been obvious.

Maybe it was one of the goddess's powers. Syssi had only a vague grasp on what Annani was capable of, and besides, she was the last person to doubt someone's special abilities. But then, if Annani's remote viewing were a real thing—a dependable source of information—Kian wouldn't have been so worried.

Apparently, the goddess was a little full of herself. Still, the last thing Syssi wanted to do was to challenge her conviction. If this misguided belief in her superpowers eased her, let her cling to it.

"I see," she said with a nod as if she'd accepted the explanation.

Annani wasn't fooled, though. "Kian is a skeptic. That is why he does not trust my visions, but I have a proven record of accurate remote viewings. And on top of those, I have a little of your talent, though in my case it is more of a gut feeling than a vision."

"Sometimes it's hard to tell the difference," Syssi admitted. "And your gut tells you no one will get hurt?"

"I did not say that. I just know that there will be no carnage tonight. And I am basing this on more than just my gut."

"Like what?" *That should be interesting.*

"As I said, I believe Amanda is in control of the situation, and the Doomer will not hurt her. As to the men on the team, they not only outnumber him six to one, but also have the element of surprise on their side."

"And what about the Doomer himself? What are his chances of getting out of this alive?" Syssi sincerely doubted the possibility. Kian intended to kill the guy. Otherwise, why carry a sword?

"His chances are good. I forbid unnecessary killings."

"What do you mean?"

"Exactly what I said. If an enemy is killed during a life and death fight, then his death is sanctioned. But I do not allow the execution of a subdued captive." Annani lifted her chin as if expecting Syssi to object.

In theory, Annani's approach was the morally right thing to do. Except, if they didn't kill enemy warriors, what did they do with the men they captured?

Kian hadn't mentioned any war prisoners being held in the clan's jail even though some Doomers must've been captured recently. The guardians who'd defended both her and Michael from Doomers' attack had most likely taken some of their assailants prisoner. And if they had, where were they?

"I wasn't aware of any enemy prisoners being

held down in your basement."

"Oh, Kian told you about the jail? I did not know that. But no, they are not in the jail. They are kept in the crypt."

Crypt? Like a burial chamber?

"I don't understand, you said they are taken alive…"

"Only barely. You see, an immortal can be held in stasis indefinitely. Which means a state in between, like the undead from your lore." Annani chuckled.

"How is it possible?"

"It is a precise art. The victim has to be injected with venom to a point when his heart slows down to almost nothing but still beats—a little more would kill him, a little less and he will revive in short order, regenerating his injuries."

"And that's what you order the Guardians to do?"

"Exactly. We call it injecting to the brink. Then we store them in the crypt." Annani looked like she had just revealed a most clever and marvelous plan.

"Why? What do you plan to do with them?"

Annani's face fell a little. "It is the same question Kian keeps asking me. He does not agree with my decree, and he chafes at having to obey it."

Annani sighed. "But I just cannot allow it. There are so few of our kind left, and that includes the Doomers. I would be contributing to my own people's extinction if I let it happen. At this time, I have no solution for how to salvage these men. They have been brainwashed since birth and we do not have the resources and manpower to rehabilitate them or keep them as prisoners. So I did the only thing I could think of. I will keep them in stasis for as long as their leadership continues on its destructive path. But if one day something happens to Navuh, hopefully a coup, and the Brotherhood changes its objectives, maybe then I could order them revived."

"Your heart is so full of love... " Syssi said, when something occurred to her. "Are you by any chance the goddess of love?" Annani was, after all, ancient, and who was to say that she wasn't the mythological Venus? Or Aphrodite? Or Ishtar? Or any of the other names different cultures attached to the ideal of love and beauty?

"Maybe I am..." Annani winked.

She was kidding, right?

"Speaking of love, tell me how did you and Kian meet, and when did you fall in love? I adore a good love story. Especially when it involves my precious son."

Was Annani deflecting cleverly? Or did she just enjoy being mysterious? In any case, it wasn't like Syssi could pressure her for an answer.

"Well?" Annani motioned with a wave of her hand.

"We met at Amanda's lab at the university. Kian came to try to convince her it wasn't safe for her to stay there after the Doomers had murdered that programmer. She, of course, refused to listen to reason. But then his bodyguards called to warn about Doomers outside the lab, and he whisked us both away and brought us here."

"And what did you think of him when you first saw him? I want all the juicy details, not just the dry facts." Annani's eyes sparkled with excitement.

The goddess apparently not only looked like a teenager but had the mentality to match.

Syssi chuckled. "I thought he looked too good for a mere mortal, and I was right because as it turned out he wasn't."

Annani scooted on her chair to get closer. "Was it love at first sight? Did you know right away that he was the one?"

More like lust at first sight... Not that she was going to admit it to Annani. "I thought he was out of my league and tried to hide behind my computer monitor. I didn't want him to see me."

"Why on earth not? You are beautiful!"

"Thank you. But I'm well aware that compared to Kian and Amanda I'm just ordinary. Anyway, for some reason Kian walked over to my station and forced me to show myself." Syssi shrugged, pretending as if it had been nothing special when, in fact, she had almost fainted. And when he had taken her hand, she'd almost orgasmed just from that one little touch. But again, it was not something she wished to share with Kian's mother.

Except, judging by the knowing smirk on Annani's beautiful face, Syssi had a feeling the goddess wasn't fooled by her feigned nonchalance.

Annani sighed. "Oh, well, I see that you are uncomfortable sharing the exciting details with me. But at least tell me how it happened."

Thank God! That I can do.

"After we got to his apartment, Amanda made up a story to explain why we had to run. She told me that the attackers were some religious fanatics who believed our work was evil and had threatened her before. We had a drink and Kian took me home. Once we got there, he thralled me to forget everything that had happened, including himself, and sent me off to sleep." *But not before he kissed me senseless.*

"Then the next morning he showed up on my

doorstep, introduced himself as Amanda's brother, and said I needed to come away with him. When I hesitated, he returned my memories."

"That must have been very confusing for you," Annani said.

"It was. I thought I was losing my mind. But anyway, he took me to his place and that was it."

Annani arched one perfect red brow. "That was when you fell in love with him?"

Syssi blushed. "I've been attracted to Kian from the first moment I saw him, but then any normal woman would be. He is so handsome and so impressive. But I realized that I loved him only after I got to know him better and discovered what a sweet and wonderful person he is."

Annani beamed like the proud mother she was. "Just do not ever tell him you think of him as sweet. I think my son will take offense."

Syssi chuckled. "I know. He is like a prickly pear, thorny on the outside, but sweet on the inside, and he doesn't want anyone to know he has a softer side."

Annani nodded. "As a leader, he is required to project strength and authority. Sweet will not cut it."

"No, I guess not."

CHAPTER 23: KIAN

*T*rekking through the sparse forest on foot, Kian cursed. He hated that he was forced to slow down and wait for the mortals to catch up. Again.

He and the brothers could have been at the cabin by now.

It wasn't that the humans were out of shape or took it easy... they were simply outclassed...

Which seemed to rub Andrew the wrong way. As he hurried to close the distance, the murderous expression on the guy's face was like a promise of violence.

Bring it on, buddy... let's see what you're made of... just make it quick... Every minute that passed was another minute of Amanda enduring hell. Kian's hands hovered over his weapons, ready to disarm fast... Because if he accidentally killed the human...

Calm the fuck up... he is Syssi's brother... he is Syssi's brother... a good guy...

Kian took a deep breath and moved his hands behind his back, holding on tight.

"What the hell are you trying to prove, Kian? That you're faster? Stronger?" Andrew got in his face. "Well, fucking great for you."

Almost touching chests, Kian stared Andrew down from his superior height. "You'd better adjust your attitude, buddy."

Andrew didn't back down. "You are sabotaging the mission, dumbass!"

No one talked to Kian like that.

"Only Syssi's concern for you stays my fist from rearranging your face," he hissed through lengthening fangs as he took a step into Andrew.

"Holy fuck..." Andrew took a step back. "You are one scary motherfucker, aren't you?" Lifting his hand, he got closer again and reached a finger to touch one of Kian's fangs. "You're not fucking with my head this time, are you? Those things are like what? Two inches long? And your eyes... holy shit... they are glowing like a pair of fucking flashlights..."

Kian shook his head. Evidently, his future

brother-in-law was insane. Anyone with any sense of self-preservation would have been at least cautious if not terrified by that display.

But not Andrew, there was no fear in the guy's scent. Not a trace.

"And you must be one of those psychos who get a hard-on from an adrenaline rush."

"Hold your horses." Anandur butted his head in between them, his crinkly beard scratching Kian's forehead. "Until you ladies are done complimenting each other, Brundar and I are going to take a piss, and we are taking Rodney and the other one with us. Do us all a favor and either kiss and make up or beat the crap out of each other, but get over yourselves." He flicked them both on the top of their heads before turning around and gesturing for the rest of the men to follow. "Five minutes," he threw over his shoulder as the bunch walked away.

Kian groaned. Anandur's intervention had been like a needle prick to the overinflated balloon of his aggression. For the big oaf to step in as the voice of reason, Kian must've been doing a really piss-poor job of handling things.

Yeah, he sighed, feeling his fangs retract.

The storm in his head, the rage, the worry, the

deep-seated hatred, guilt… had clouded his head, allowing the mindless beast inside him to surface.

"You are right." Kian ran a hand through his hair, suddenly feeling a desperate need to light up. "You mind if I smoke?" He pulled the pack out of his shirt pocket.

"Not at all, but if you don't mind, I'm going to sit down." Andrew lowered himself to the ground.

After a moment, Kian followed him down. "Can I offer you one?"

"Thanks, but no. I live dangerously enough as it is." Andrew waved him off.

"That I believe." Kian chuckled as he lit up.

"I never take unnecessary risks. I don't know what gave you that impression."

"Could've fooled me." Kian exhaled a ring of smoke. "The way you got in my face, in the state I was in, wasn't smart. You saw me; I'm more beast than man when I get like that."

"Nah, I knew you wouldn't do anything to me."

"What if I was too far gone? You know next to nothing about me and my kind and what to expect from us."

"That's where you are wrong. I might not know exactly what you are, but I do know who you are. And anyway, I knew I could count on that redheaded Goliath to jump in if needed."

"Goliath... ha? I like it. Usually, I just call him a big oaf."

"Is he?"

"Nah, but he likes to pretend he is." In the silence that followed, Kian concentrated on the rings of smoke he was making. It was a little like meditating, relaxing.

"We agreed that it would be best for me to lead the mission. You need to slow the fuck down and let me set the pace. Got it?"

"Yeah."

"Wow, miracles do happen. I expected you to give me more crap over this."

"No, I have no problem admitting when I'm wrong." Kian pushed up to his feet and offered a hand-up to Andrew. "Though don't expect an apology..."

"Wouldn't dream of it." The man took what he was offered and pulled himself up, slapping Kian's shoulder before he let go.

"Oh, how touching. You girls made up. I have tears in my eyes." Anandur sniffled, placing a hand over his heart and batting his eyelashes.

Two hands flicked his head at the same time as Kian and Andrew got him between them.

Patting his messed-up curls, Anandur groaned, "I feel the love."

CHAPTER 24: SHARIM

As the island's transport reached flight altitude, Sharim pulled out the stack of fake passports he and his two companions would be using on their way to Los Angeles.

Going over the different names he'd chosen for himself, he devised a little trick to remember who he was supposed to be on each leg of the trip. After all, it would look pretty suspicious for him to respond with a *huh?* Or a *what?* Or not at all, when addressed as Mr. So-and-so.

The trick was quite simple; he created a little backstory for each name and a character to go with it. Modeling the four made-up versions of himself either on men he knew or characters in films, he made a movie in his head. Each had not only a unique posture, his own hand gestures, and individual syntax and inflection, but also a completely disparate personality.

He chose the version he liked best to go with the name he decided to use throughout the remainder of this mission.

Sharim would become Sebastian Shar—a wealthy businessman looking to invest in movies, radio stations, and newspapers. A charming, easygoing Australian everyone liked. Especially the ladies...

Until they discovered his true nature, that is. Sharim chuckled.

Not that he planned on seducing any of his future female business associates. He'd flirt, of course, but only because it would help his interests. Many of the media industry executives were female, and his charm was an asset he planned on utilizing to its fullest.

In order to protect the image of his manufactured persona, though, his twisted preferences would have to be kept not only private but secret. If word got out regarding his sexual activities, it would have disastrous consequences on his business dealings. Until he got his hands on at least one piece of young flesh and had her imprisoned in the dungeon he was planning to build for just this purpose, he'd have to limit himself to escort services that specialized in his kind of kink. But the best solution was to renew his membership to that fancy BDSM club downtown. Tormenting willing partners was not as fun, but in the meantime, it would have to do.

"Here." He handed the men their passports. "Memorize the names and choose the one you like best for last. From the moment we embark on the final leg of the trip to Los Angeles, our old names will be left behind. We'll be reborn with these new ones, using them exclusively even among ourselves. You'd be smart to start practicing."

The best way to create a false identity was not to act like that person, but become him. He would think as Sebastian Shar, talk as Sebastian Shar, and eventually dream as Sebastian Shar.

Waiting impatiently for the men to choose theirs, he was eager to begin the game. But the guys were just simple soldiers, and although the two were fairly intelligent and capable, they had none of his special skills. Not to mention that he'd had a millennium of practice to perfect them that the much younger immortals hadn't.

Still, waiting patiently for others to catch up wasn't a skill he had full mastery of, yet.

The guys kept flipping between the dark booklets. Judging by their frowns and head-shaking, it appeared to be a tough choice to make.

His second was the first to be done. After tucking one of the passports in his shoulder bag, he inserted the others inside a special compartment in his suitcase.

"Robert Dowson." He offered his hand to Sharim.

"Sebastian Shar. It's a pleasure to make your acquaintance, Robert."

"The pleasure is all mine, Mr. Shar."

"Please, call me Sebastian."

"Yes, sir."

"You have to lose the *Yes sir*, Robert. And that rigid spine has to go as well. From now on you're not a soldier, but a corporate executive. Act like one."

"Yes, sir."

Sebastian rolled his eyes. "You want to try that again?"

"No problem."

"That's better." He wondered how long it would take until Robert would walk the walk and talk the talk...

The good news was that he expected the other guy to do better. His assistant was young, sharp, and liked watching a lot of American movies and goofing around.

The boy didn't disappoint.

"Damn, Sebastian. I wanted to be Robert. I asked you to put me down as Robert Downey Jr., but instead, you gave it to a guy that has no idea who the hell it is."

"It's bad enough that you look like that actor's doppelgänger. Using a similar name would've made you a caricature, not a real person. You feel me?"

"Yeah, I get it. But why did you have to give it to him?" He pointed at the tall soldier who looked nothing like the actor.

"So you'd be sure to remember it."

"Oh, hell, Tom Carson it is, then."

"Nice to meet you, Tom."

"Yeah, same here, but I still don't know who that Tom is supposed to be. Any suggestions?"

"You're fine as you are. You're an assistant to a successful businessman, and your flippant attitude is tolerated because you're so incredibly good at what you do."

The guy smiled, showing a lot of white teeth, and dipped his head in an impression of a bow. "Thank you, I appreciate the compliment, Sebastian."

"It's all settled then. Let's go over the travel plan one more time before we land."

The airports he'd chosen for the layovers were big and located in countries that had no reason to invest in face recognition technology.

Just in case.

Hopping from one airport to another and then taking a bus or train ride through Europe, they would each take different routes until they met again in Munich. They would travel the last leg of the trip on the same plane, but they wouldn't be sitting together.

Sebastian's route would take him from Kuala Lumpur to Sydney, then from Sydney to Istanbul. Flying first class, he would spend some of the twenty plus hours of that flight sleeping, so he would be fresh and ready to have a good time in Prague, which was his next destination. From there, it would be a bus to Munich, and then a direct flight to Los Angeles.

CHAPTER 25: DALHU

*D*alhu wrapped the sleeves of his dress shirt around Amanda's wrists and tied the ends in a loose bow.

"Make it tighter," Amanda commanded.

He did it again, a little snugger this time. "I think this is good enough. Any tighter and it will constrict your circulation."

The irony of Amanda still calling the shots, even in how she wanted to be restrained, wasn't lost on him. He didn't mind, though.

Their first time was going to be all about her.

He was going to pleasure her like she'd never been pleasured before, have her climb higher than she ever had, and erase the memory of all those mortals she'd bedded before him.

"You think?" Amanda gave a tug, and the whole thing fell apart.

"I have an idea. How about I tie it around your mouth instead of your hands? It will be more conducive to what you have in mind."

He was only half joking.

"Yeah, you might have a point. I'm being too bossy. Do it."

Now, that was hilarious... especially since she wasn't trying to be funny...

With the shirt wadded in his hand, he stretched on top of her, pinning her down with his weight. For a moment, he just gazed at her stunning face. Then he kissed her, licking at the seam between her lips, penetrating her mouth, tasting, taking...

Groaning, she gave as good as she got, her nails digging into his neck to hold him to her, her legs parting to welcome him between them.

Was he the luckiest male on the planet? Or what?

And then she started to grind against him.

Oh, hell, he wasn't going to last like that.

With an effort, he released her mouth, taking a moment to collect himself before lifting his head to look into Amanda's glowing blue eyes.

So feral—so clearly not human.

Hers were the eyes of a hungry predator—a

tigress, a cougar—challenging her male to prove himself worthy...

"I'm not going to cover these lush lips of yours. I have plans for them." He smiled down at her. "Give me your hands."

Pushing back, he braced on his knees and straddled her narrow waist. Holding her wrists with one hand, he wrapped the shirtsleeves around them—this time utilizing a serious knot—the kind he would have used on a prisoner...

Well, almost. There was a big difference between the luxurious fabric of his expensive dress shirt and a coarse rope...

"Try it now, princess." He smirked as she gave it a tug, then another one, stronger this time, and still the knot held. "You think you can get out of that?" he taunted.

"I bet I could if I needed to. But it's good." She sighed, stretching her arms over her head, her whole body loosening in surrender.

It finally dawned on him then.

Up until that moment, he'd assumed she was playing a game, amusing herself with something she hadn't experienced before.

But that wasn't what this was about.

Not at all.

This was about Amanda giving herself permission to let go. And she couldn't do so until it was out of her hands… literally.

Leaning back on his haunches, Dalhu gazed at all that magnificent beauty sprawled before him like an offering and felt unbelievably lucky.

Privileged.

The whole thing seemed unreal.

"You're so beautiful," he murmured, though what he really meant to say was *thank you*. And not only to Amanda, but to the Fates, or the universe, or whatever higher power had granted such a gift to someone as undeserving as him.

Hooded with passion, her eyes lingered on his face for a brief moment before going on a slow and deliberate tour of every muscle in his body. "You're not so bad yourself," she said.

Kind of made a guy feel eight feet tall. Not that his height wasn't impressive to begin with, but yeah…

In a sinuous wave, he lowered himself on top of her, and bracing his elbows by her sides, cupped her face in his palms.

She parted her lips, inviting him to take her mouth again.

He kissed her slow and deep. Moving one palm to encircle her throat, he kissed and nipped his way down her jawline to the spot on her neck where her pulse was beating fast between his splayed fingers.

Pulling in a ragged breath through her teeth, Amanda let loose a small whimper and turned her head in his gentle hold, providing him with more expanse of soft skin to kiss and nip at.

As he ran his lips down and up the column of her neck, his fangs scraping lightly against her skin, she shivered, though not because she was afraid. She trusted him... and he realized that by closing his hand over her throat he'd been testing her.

And what a heady feeling that was. Her trust was something he hadn't dared hope for, despite being compelled to seek it.

Sliding down, he released Amanda's throat, his palm drifting to her breast. He had neglected these beauties, letting them get chilled in the cold cabin, and it was about time he remedied this situation. Cupping his hand over one, he dipped his head and used his mouth to warm the other.

Amanda moaned, bucking up into him, and that was even before he began doing anything interesting. Which was about to change as soon as he deemed her perky breasts sufficiently warmed, starting with the one already in his mouth. Putting his tongue to work, he swirled it around the tight little nub, flicking and licking at it before giving it a hard pull as he hollowed his cheeks and sucked it in.

Then he did it again on her other side while his fingers paid attention to the one he'd just released. At first, he only circled his thumb round and round the wet, turgid peak. But then, as he got serious about the sucking and the nipping on the other side, he caught her sensitive flesh between his thumb and finger. Pinching and tweaking, he increased the pressure he applied, gauging Amanda's response by her moans and the increased tempo of her gyrations.

The wild cat was loving it, and he would've lingered feasting on her breasts if he weren't so eager to get his mouth on another part of her anatomy.

Like right now...

Sliding even farther down her body, he kissed her belly button, then swirled the tip of his tongue inside it while his hands got busy with the button of her jeans. The zipper was next, and as he pulled it down a little bit at a time, he licked a trail down to the line of her pink cotton panties.

Surprisingly, it was one of the simple ones he'd picked for her in the general store, and not a fancy new one from the selection he'd bought for her at that lingerie store, or rather Plain Jane had. But he knew there was an even better surprise waiting for him under that cotton. Amanda was completely bare—he'd glimpsed it when he'd seen her in all her naked glory in that bathtub upstairs. Dalhu wondered if this was natural for a female of his kind or had she had it removed. In either case, he found it hot as hell. Imagining how soft and smooth that most intimate female flesh would feel under his lips and his tongue, he was impatient to get to it.

It was good then that her jeans were the kind that stretched; otherwise he would have torn them at the seams in his mad rush to yank them off Amanda's slender legs. The pink panties joined the ride and got tossed to the floor together with what had covered them. A split second later, he had his palm over what was his gateway to heaven.

Oh, man, the heat...

And she was so wet... drenched...

His mouth watered as he dipped his head to take his first taste.

As his long and dexterous tongue licked a path from the fountain of all that heavenly nectar up to the top of her wet folds—to the place where the key to her treasure was hidden—Amanda growled. The sound was more like that of a feral cat than a woman—the kind that would've scared a lesser man—a mortal.

Diving in for more of that ambrosia, he wondered if she'd ever made that sound for anyone but him...

The thought of his woman with some puny, weak human spurred his aggression, and his need to get inside her, to penetrate her became over-whelming...

He did...

With his tongue.

Shaping it into a spear, he thrust it deep inside her, penetrating her as he would with his shaft, fucking her rhythmically, forcefully. His palms clamped on her butt cheeks, he held her in place while he tongue-fucked her...

No... damn it.

He was supposed to be making love to his woman, not fucking her. And even though the difference was only in how he phrased it in his head, it struck him as a kind of sacrilege.

Fuck!

Damn it, he was starting to hate that word...

Even if it killed him, he was going to make love to Amanda slowly, tenderly—his body an exten-sion of his heart.

Dialing back on his aggression, he began lapping leisurely.

Amanda's animal groans soon tapered down to a more human sounding moan, and she cranked her head up to get a better view of what he was doing.

Hot damn.

His mouth and nose buried between her wet folds, he gazed up at her eyes.

Seeing her beautiful face framed by the pair of her glorious breasts, flushed with lust as she watched him pleasuring her, was so fucking hot that he was afraid his mind would short-circuit.

As it was, his fangs reached their full length, pulsating with the urgent need to be sunk into his female whether his shaft was inside her or not.

"Do it," she breathed.

Oh, man, was he tempted. Licking a spot at the juncture of her inner thigh, he felt Amanda shiver in anticipation, the slight scent of her fear doing nothing to cool him down—on the contrary.

He was, after all, a predator, and for the first time in his long life he didn't have to wrestle with his nature to avoid hurting a female.

Amanda was not only just as feral as he, but she was practically indestructible.

Not to mention that after all her puny, mortal,

boy toy lovers, she must crave that which only he could give her.

But biting her would be cheating, wouldn't it?

He wanted to make her climax before the venom did the work for him. And not just climax; he wanted her to fly higher than she had ever flown before and fall apart all over him, screaming his name. Or moaning it, or whispering it…

Whatever… as long as it was his name.

"Not yet, I want to make you come first… over…and…over…again…" he said in between long, wet laps of his tongue.

"Oh, hell…" She groaned and dropped back, the outpour of wetness he caught with his tongue the best kind of *yes* imaginable.

CHAPTER 26: KIAN

*T*rekking behind Andrew, Kian gritted his teeth. Despite the fact that they were nearing their destination well ahead of time, the easy pace the guy was dictating was driving him insane.

Kian was well aware that his irritation was irrational, but he couldn't help it.

He was losing it big time.

Thankfully, it wasn't long before the cabin's steep roof came into view, and a few moments later Andrew motioned for them to halt.

The plan was for Kian and the brothers to wait some distance away from the cabin while Andrew and his buddies went ahead and planted small explosives around its perimeter. No need to risk the Doomer's innate immortal-male-alert waking him up prematurely, and ruin the tactical advantage of a surprise attack.

Hopefully, the fucker was a sound sleeper and wouldn't detect the faint scent emitted by the mortals. And besides, with the wind picking up, odds were that their scent would disperse before it had a chance to filter through the cabin's walls.

Not that it had done any good with the rest of the creatures inhabiting the forest. Judging by the howling frenzy of a nearby wolf pack, the wind wasn't all that effective in taking care of their team's smell. The fucking wolves were not only aware of the interlopers' presence, but the pack had been stealthily following them for some time now, getting vocal at the most inopportune time.

Unfortunately, as careful and as detailed as Andrew's plan was, there was no way to factor in nature's hindrance or conversely assistance.

Damn. Hopefully, the howling wouldn't alert the Doomer.

As Andrew led the group behind the cover of a slightly denser growth, he shrugged off his backpack and leaned it against the heavy roots of a tree. Crouching next to the green army issue, he pulled out a laser range meter and pointed it toward the cabin, took the measurement, then pointed it toward a large outcropping some five hundred yards away. "Kian, I need to time your guys' speed out here. Every fraction of a second counts. When I give the signal, I want you to sprint to that big rock over there." He motioned toward the rock formation. "It's the same distance from us as the cabin."

Readying for the next stage of the plan to commence, Kian's muscles were already coiled. "All three of us at once, or one at a time?"

"One at a time."

"I'll go first."

"Wait for my signal... And go!" As Andrew pressed a button on his watch, a corresponding red light flashed on Kian's.

He crossed the distance in seconds.

"Damn, you're fast," Andrew said as he recorded the time. "Okay, now you." He pointed at Anandur. "Go!"

Then it was Brundar's turn.

"And the winner is..." Andrew pointed at Kian.

Apparently, adrenaline had given him a boost. Kian had expected Brundar to win—the guy was their fastest runner.

"And you guys are not even breathing hard. Amazing." Andrew shook his head. "Okay, listen up. I'm going to go over the details again."

"No need." Kian waved him off.

"Maybe yes, maybe not. But you're going to listen anyway."

Kian rolled his eyes but said nothing. Arguing with Andrew was pointless, and besides, he'd given his word that he would not interfere and would let the guy lead.

"Once the explosives are in place, I'll give the go signal, and you guys sprint for the cabin. Fifteen seconds later, I'll detonate the explosives. The timing is crucial. I timed your speed and calculated exactly how many seconds it takes you to cross the distance. The explosives will detonate precisely three seconds before you guys reach the cabin."

In addition to blowing a hole in the wall for unobstructed entry, the explosions would create a distraction, going off simultaneously in several spots around the perimeter and, hopefully, disorienting the Doomer.

If everything happened exactly as planned, the commotion would distract the fucker long enough for Kian to get to him before the Doomer had a chance to grab Amanda and put a knife to her throat.

Then it would be game over.

The Doomer was Kian's.

CHAPTER 27: AMANDA

*H*oly hell.

The best sexual experience of her life, and this was just the foreplay. While expertly playing her body to a fever pitch with his mouth, Dalhu had kept his pants on, and she could only imagine how amazing that hard length she'd felt before through his jeans would feel inside her.

Amanda had expected sex with an immortal male to be different, but this was on a level she couldn't have even conceived.

In comparison, her prior experiences couldn't even qualify as masturbation.

What was it that cranked the dial on the erotic gauge all the way up? Immortal male's pheromones at work? The right chemistry? Was it Dalhu's magnificently powerful body?

Holding her in place, making her feel feminine, delicate, fragile...

Dominating her...

Gently, reverently...

The combination was so fucking hot—the novelty of being with a male who could overpower her with ease and yet never would without her permission.

Who knew that a male's dominance could be such a turn-on?

Well, not just any male, but still...

Even though Dalhu was more than strong enough to subdue her without tying her up, and even though she could've gotten free if she wished so, the make-believe restraint allowed her to give herself over to the pleasure. For once, she was allowing a male to take the lead and not thinking of what would be her next move.

Amanda didn't have even one submissive bone in her body, and though not quite the dominatrix, she was used to being the one in charge.

Maybe this was it. Maybe it was so hot because this was all new to her.

Different.

It felt like a new beginning.

A fresh start.

All thoughts ceased as she felt his thick finger

slowly penetrating her. First one, then two… and as he began pumping, her body surged up to meet his lips.

He clamped a hand on her thigh, holding her down as he licked around her clitoris, his fingers moving in and out in maddeningly shallow thrusts.

She shifted up and heard herself say a word she'd never said during sex before."Pleeeease…"

Dalhu growled as he lifted his head. "Please what?"

His eyes glowing and his fangs fully extended, he looked feral, and instinctively, she knew the time to truly surrender was now. Behind those wild eyes, she saw little, if any, of the man. The beast had taken over, and it couldn't care less that she was impatient for him to bring her to a climax, and it certainly had never heard of women's lib.

The beast was asserting its dominance as it claimed its female.

Damn, it was hot.

As her body responded with an outpour of wetness, Amanda let her head drop back. Perhaps there was a little submissive bone somewhere in there after all.

Nah… Not me…

But as Dalhu kept her at a near boiling simmer, growling and nipping at her inner thighs whenever she wouldn't hold still, the coil inside her was winding impossibly tighter.

Amanda held on.

He wasn't going to let her come before he was good and ready, and once he did, she was going to shoot through the roof.

At first, the desperate sounds she was making— the mewls and the growls and the keening moans —embarrassed her. But as it became almost painful to be held over that elusive edge, she stopped thinking and let herself go wild. She didn't care anymore if Dalhu heard the tortured sounds he was wringing out of her, or that her head was thrashing side to side as her bound hands banged on the armrest.

Letting it all loose was liberating.

It felt amazing.

She was burning, and with her the whole world was going up in flames.

Let it burn. She didn't care.

Then Dalhu thrust his incredibly long fingers all the way inside her and curled them against that sweet spot on her front wall, at the same time sucking her clit between his lips, hard.

The orgasm exploded from her with the force of a volcanic eruption, and she screamed his name as she flew, soaring above as it went spewing out like lava, on and on, until there was nothing left inside her.

And with her, all around her, the world was exploding.

Boom! Boom! Boom!

Boom!

CHAPTER 28: ANDREW

$\mathcal{A}$ ndrew cleared the tree line and stopped. The cabin had approximately a hundred feet of open space around it, with only one mature oak in front to provide cover. But as he'd expected, the place was mostly dark. All but the two uppermost windows were shuttered, and some dim light was visible through those two small triangles of glass. Still, with the moonlight finally breaking through the heavy cover of clouds, the illumination was sufficient for him to take off his night-vision goggles.

Behind him, Jake and Rodney did the same.

He'd left the immortals who needed no help with night vision some distance away, where the forest was denser and provided better cover.

Stronger, faster, and the bastards can see perfectly in

the dark.

Well, good for them. Hopefully, they could also do something about that bloody wolf pack because the fucking howling was getting on his nerves.

And what's worse, the wind was picking up at an alarming rate, which might render the helicopter useless for the return trip.

Fuck! Like he needed another complication.

He'd better hurry and assess the situation inside that cabin.

It would've been great if the immortals could also see through walls, but unlike Superman, they didn't have that ability.

Bummer, it could've saved him some time.

He would need to get close and check.

After all, it wouldn't be much of a rescue if they placed the explosives next to where Amanda was sleeping and blew her up. Though, if luck would have it, the perp was sleeping right next to a wall.

As Andrew approached the east side of the structure, he carefully lowered his heavy backpack to the ground, then pulled out the portable Xaver 800 Electromagnetic Radar. The thing was not as easy to operate as the smaller models, requiring a tripod, but it provided the most accurate picture of a room's interior, including placement of furniture, the exact location of live occupants, and their movements. With the tripod's legs extended, he placed the device next to the wall and turned it on.

Fucking hell.

The good news was that he had two live ones in there, which meant Amanda was okay. The bad news was that they were together... busy... and unless that Doomer was performing a medical exam, they were doing the horizontal mambo... And it didn't seem as if Amanda was struggling either...

Golly gee-fuckin'-whiz.

Thank God, Kian couldn't see through walls. No one would've been able to stop the guy.

If not for Andrew's many years of training, he would've been no better than Syssi's hotheaded boyfriend and would've charged inside himself.

This complicated everything. Not only was the perp awake, but it would be next to impossible to get to Amanda before the guy grabbed her.

At least the sofa he had Amanda on was practically in the middle of the room so the explosives could go wherever on the perimeter of the cabin.

Circling his finger, Andrew gave the sign for Rodney and Jake to go ahead and place the things at the spots they deemed best—no impediments to point out.

By the time he was finished folding the tripod

and packing the Xaver in his backpack, the guys had everything in place. His men were the best.

Hefting the heavy load over his shoulders, he joined his buddies as they backed away, reluctantly clearing the stage for the immortals to do their thing.

They couldn't have been more than a few feet away from the cabin when he heard the scream. An ear-piercing sound that carried over the whistling wind and the howling wolves and straight into her brother's ears.

Fuck. Here goes the plan—

There was a terrifying roar, and as he fumbled with the remote-control detonator, Andrew had the impression of something hurtling toward him with the speed of a runaway car and the force of a locomotive.

No time to double-check the timing, he pressed the button and prayed to God the explosives would detonate before Kian reached the cabin.

A split second later, the explosions shook the structure behind him, and the three immortal titans passed him and his buddies, almost knocking them over as they galloped at what was an unbelievable speed even for them—they must've been faster than cheetahs.

Immortal or not, the perp was a dead man.

CHAPTER 29: KIAN

The fucker is torturing Amanda!

Racing for the cabin, Kian felt like crossing that distance was taking forever, though it couldn't have been more than a few seconds.

And yet, as fast as he was running, his mind was going even faster.

Planning.

First, he was going to tear the Doomer's throat out.

With that out of the way, he'd make sure Amanda was safe before taking out of Andrew's hide every ounce of pain Amanda had suffered because he'd been dragging his feet. While Andrew was pacing them and forcing Kian to go slow, Amanda had been tortured.

Damn, he should have listened to his gut when

it had urged him to push forward as fast as he could.

As he leaped over the smoking debris at the bottom of the large hole in the wall, the scene unfolding before him was even worse than what he'd been expecting.

Crouching with his arms spread wide and his elongated fangs dripping venom, the Doomer was trying to block the view of Amanda's nude body laid out on the couch behind him.

The fucker had her wrists tied with some rags, and although Kian couldn't see any bruises, it looked like she was passed out.

This vile creature has tied and raped my little sister.

He is going to die... painfully.

With a roar, Kian attacked.

He expected the Doomer to rush ahead and use the momentum to add power to the clash, but the fucker didn't budge from his spot, waiting for Kian to come to him.

If he thought Kian would hesitate to tear him apart in front of Amanda, he was dead wrong. Very. Dead. Wrong.

But something was off.

On impact, the huge Doomer barely moved an inch, and Kian was starting to realize that he'd underestimated his opponent. But he couldn't count on Brundar and Anandur's help because he'd given them orders not to. They'd been assigned the important task of safeguarding Amanda.

And yet, besides keeping his neck out of reach of Kian's snapping fangs, the monster did nothing more than defend himself.

And guard Amanda.

But as the brothers circled around, approaching the couch from behind, the Doomer's attention was diverted for just long enough to provide Kian with the opening he needed, and he sank his fangs into the fucker's thick neck.

Kian's intention wasn't the merciful venom killing, though, not for this monster. He was going to rip out the fucker's throat, and as the Doomer was bleeding, go for his heart.

"Nooooo!"

Amanda's shrill scream was followed by the sound of ripping fabric, and then she was on Kian's back, clutching his torso between her naked thighs and pulling on his hair with both hands.

"Don't you dare harm him! Pull your fangs out of his throat! Now!"

She was ripping his fucking hair out, pulling on it with all her strength.

What the fuck?

"And do it slowly," she hissed in his ear. "If even

a little of his skin tears... I'm never going to forgive you. Ever!"

Classic Stockholm syndrome...

Still, Kian did as she demanded. And not only because he believed she would deliver on her promise. He couldn't put his finger on it, but something was off with the scenario he'd created in his head.

"Why are you defending him? That monster had tied you down, tortured you, or raped you, or both, until you screamed and passed out from the pain." Kian held on to the Doomer, who stopped struggling.

"Not pain, you moron, pleasure. I screamed because I was having the best orgasm of my life. With your vast sexual experience, I would think you should be able to distinguish between a cry of pain and a cry of pleasure."

"But he had you tied up..."

Amanda got off his back and faced him, assuming her angry pose of hands on her hips and a foot tapping the floor.

With one significant difference—this time, she was doing it butt naked.

"It was a shirt. It took me how long to rip it apart? A second? You think I could be restrained with a piece of fabric?"

"I don't understand…"

"Really? Oh, wow, I never thought I'd have to explain sex games to you, Kian."

"Oh…"

Kian was speechless as he attempted to process what she was telling him. Everything that felt off from the moment he had leaped into this room was starting to make sense.

There had been no bruises on her because the Doomer hadn't been abusing her. She had been having sex with that scum, willingly. And as incomprehensible as it was, the fucker hadn't attacked because he'd been protecting Amanda from perceived danger and then held back when he realized it was her family who'd come to rescue her.

Fucking unbelievable.

Amanda had a lot of explaining to do, and hopefully, it was along the lines of letting the scum touch her to prevent him from killing her… not because she'd wanted it.

Though, the way she'd protected that filth, she must have developed feelings for him.

Fucking hell.

Standing naked in a room full of males, Amanda was still glaring at him. It didn't faze the brothers, but the humans were staring at her with gaping, drooling mouths.

And that included Andrew.

"Get dressed, Amanda," Kian hissed, getting up and turning away from her.

Right now, he couldn't see the beauty the others were admiring.

Amanda disgusted him.

"Anandur, slap some cuffs on the scum. He is coming with us. And bag that laptop."

Leaving them all behind, on his way out Kian stepped over the debris and marched downhill toward the spot where the helicopter was supposed to be waiting for them. It was all he could do not to say—in front of a crowd—things Amanda would never be able to forgive.

Once they were alone, though, he was going to tell her exactly what he thought of her.

CHAPTER 30: AMANDA

*T*his was bad.

No, it was good—she was getting her old life back. But there was no place for Dalhu in it. And that was bad.

Ignoring Kian's order to get dressed, Amanda crouched over Dalhu instead. Slumped on the floor with his back propped against the sofa, his arms flopped uselessly at his sides. He wasn't moving.

He looked wasted.

But although his eyes were heavy-lidded, he didn't look venom-drugged or euphoric.

He looked defeated. Drained.

"Are you okay?" she whispered, aware of the five sets of eyes trained on her naked ass.

"It's over," he whispered back. "You are free,

and I'm dead whether your people kill me or not. Just let them do it. It would be a mercy. There is no point for me to go on without you."

"Don't talk like that. Nothing is over until it's over. I'll figure something out."

"Even if you decide you want to keep me, they will never allow it. I saw how he looked at me."

"Who? Kian?"

"Yes."

"He was just angry. He thought you'd been hurting me. Once I explain what was going on, everything will be okay. Don't worry about it."

"You're wrong. You've explained and he believed you, but he still wanted me dead. And I saw the disgust in his eyes when he looked at you. Like you were dirty because I've touched you."

Yeah, she had seen it too. Not that Kian's reaction surprised her, but still, it hurt.

"He'll get over it. He always forgives me, no matter what I do."

"Not this time."

"He has no choice. I'm his little sister."

"I'm so sorry," Dalhu whispered as he closed his eyes. "You must tell him that it was just about survival—that you did it only because I'd threatened you. I don't want you to lose your brother on my account."

Anandur cleared his throat. "Sorry to interrupt, princess, but I suggest you get dressed. We need to get moving." He touched her shoulder.

"Get up," he addressed Dalhu in a much harsher tone. "Put on your boots and a shirt. Where are your clothes?"

"They are upstairs. I'll get them," Amanda said as she picked up her things from the floor and headed for the stairs.

"Didn't your mamas teach you not to stare, boys?" she threw over her shoulder to the three humans still ogling her naked butt.

"They will stop staring if you put some clothes on." Anandur chuckled.

Loath to leave Dalhu at Anandur's mercy, Amanda hurried into the bathroom, taking only a moment to clean up with a washcloth before getting dressed. She grabbed her purse and a shirt for Dalhu on her way down.

"Here you go." She handed it to him.

Anandur waited for Dalhu to put it on and button it up before cuffing him.

He was treating Dalhu better than she would've expected, not roughing him up or shoving him, and Amanda wondered if it was because she was watching. Otherwise, Anandur probably wouldn't have been as nice.

"Let's go," he said after Dalhu pulled on his boots.

The brothers led the small group out with Dalhu between them.

Amanda tried to squeeze in, wanting to be by his side, but Anandur shook his head, and she was relegated to walking behind them.

The three humans were apparently still in a state of shock from seeing her naked because none of them said a single word as they trailed after her.

Well, they would get over it. She had bigger problems than that.

What the hell was she going to do?

She knew Kian would forbid her having any contact with Dalhu, and if she insisted, he would eventually cave in but despise her for doing it.

What a mess.

She didn't want to forsake Dalhu, especially not to her brother's merciless clutches.

Fates, Kian was probably going to torture the poor guy. Which was entirely unnecessary since Dalhu had promised to reveal everything he knew voluntarily. But Kian wouldn't believe him and would torture him anyway.

But more than that, she wasn't ready to let the little flame that had sparked between them die before it had a chance to flare.

And if she was honest with herself, that flame wasn't so small.

It wasn't that she had fallen in love or anything, but for the first time in her life, there was a chance she might.

With a Doomer...

Fates, why? Why out of all the men in the universe had they matched her with a Doomer? Was it some kind of a cosmic joke? A punishment? Was throwing the two of them together a source of amusement for the fickle Fates?

But was he even her match?

Who knew?

But after all, he was the only one out there she could have.

She felt more than saw as Andrew picked up his pace and sidled up to her.

"How are you holding up?" he asked with a sidelong glance at her face.

"Just peachy."

"I'm sorry Kian is being an ass to you, and I want you to know that I'm here for you. The whole ordeal must've been traumatic, but you've handled it beautifully. Survival justifies the use of any and every tool at your disposal. And as your beauty is your best weapon, I'm glad that you used it."

"Dalhu didn't force me. In fact, all the poor guy

did was to pleasure me. We were interrupted before we had a chance to do the deed."

"I got that. But even if you had to seduce him to gain some kind of advantage, it was still a smart move. I would've advised my own sister to do the same."

Andrew was being such a sweetheart, so supportive at a time when she really needed a friend. Amanda was loath to tell him the truth and lose that support—as well as shatter his illusions.

"I'm so sorry, Andrew." She choked a little as tears welled in her eyes. His compassion was her kryptonite, making her weak. It was easier to be strong when there was no one to lean on.

"For what?"

"You're such a nice guy. Too nice for someone like me."

"What are you talking about?" He frowned.

"I did what I did because I wanted to. Not because I was afraid for my life or because Dalhu had threatened me or demanded anything other than being given a chance to woo me. So if it proves that I'm a slut and have absolutely no self-control, so be it. I never claimed otherwise. I'm not going to apologize for it."

"I see." Andrew dropped his head, keeping his eyes on his boots as they made their way downhill.

"Do yourself a favor and forget I ever flirted with you. It meant nothing. Not that you're not a great guy, you are. But there could've never been more than a casual hookup between us. We are, um… incompatible." She took a furtive peek at his hard face.

She had no idea how much he'd been told, and as the mortals had shown up after Dalhu and Kian's fangs had already retracted, they probably had seen nothing out of the ordinary.

Well, except for her in all her naked glory.

"Syssi has turned." He pinned her with a challenging stare.

"What?" Amanda froze, halting their little procession, and turned to face him.

"Sh… keep walking." He took her elbow, propelling her forward. "I know everything, but my men are on a need to know basis only. Kian is going to scramble their memories once we get back, but the less they know, the less he will have to mess with."

"When?" she whispered.

"It started at the restaurant we all had lunch at. Syssi began feeling sick right after you left and lost consciousness during the night. They were not sure she was going to make it. Lucky for me, I didn't find out until she pulled through, otherwise

I would've tried to kill your obnoxious brother and we both know how that would've ended... Anyway, when I couldn't get a hold of her on the phone, I got worried, hoofed it to your building, and demanded to see her."

"How did you find where she was? Did you have her followed?"

"It was the necklace. I've known her location all along." He pointed to the small heart pendant Amanda was still wearing. "Syssi had no idea I had a tracking device installed inside the thing. That's how we were able to find you. You are very lucky that she gave it to you."

Amanda flashed him a sideways grin. "Or not. Dalhu grabbed me at the jewelry store where I went to have it duplicated. But be that as it may, I'm glad you're a paranoid, overprotective brother. Thank you."

"You're welcome."

For the next couple of minutes, they walked in silence. As the terrain got rougher, she stumbled a couple of times. The soles of the plain sneakers Dalhu had gotten her weren't providing much cushioning for her feet—she felt every little rock. Watching her step, she was slowing them down, and the gap between Dalhu and the Guardians and the rest of the group was widening.

"Do you want me to carry you? It seems you're suffering," Andrew offered.

Such a sweet guy.

She thought of dubbing him Andrew the Sweet, though not to his face, of course. It wouldn't sit well with his tough guy image.

Instead, she gave him an incredulous look. "Thank you. It is very sweet of you to offer. But really? You think? I'm not a small woman. I'm almost as tall as you. You'll fall, and both of us will end up tumbling down the hill. I'm fine, just being careful."

"Let me at least hold your hand. You scare the shit out of me every time you list to the side."

Rolling her eyes, she took the hand he offered. "Now that you know what I am, you should be aware that I'm not exactly fragile."

"Yes, I know. Just let me be a gentleman and deal with it."

Andrew's hand was large and warm, and his strong arm saved her from painfully twisting her ankle a few times. But for some reason, it felt awkward to hold it. He was really nice, and she liked him, but...

It felt as if she was being unfaithful... and how ridiculous was that.

Ridiculous or not, she nonetheless stretched on

her tiptoes, trying to ascertain if Dalhu and the Guardians were indeed too far away to see or hear her exchange with Andrew.

"Don't worry about losing them. I know the way." Andrew misunderstood her concern.

Well, she wasn't going to explain what she was worried about—he would think she had lost her freaking mind. "I'm not worried. So, how is Syssi taking it? Being immortal, I mean."

"I don't think she's had time to process it yet. Right when she got back on her feet, she had to deal with your kidnapping and us going on a rescue mission."

"It seems that I always manage to steal the spotlight, providing all the drama and excitement. But at least it's never boring with me around. Right?" She grimaced.

"Of that I'm sure," Andrew's voice dropped, and he squeezed her hand, his hard face softening as he regarded her...

Fondly...

Fondly wasn't the right word for what she saw in his eyes, but she was going to stick with it anyway.

"Kian offered to activate my dormant genes..." Andrew glanced at her from under his long lashes.

That's right, she hadn't thought of that. As

Syssi's brother, Andrew was also a Dormant. Her brain must've turned into mush. But who could blame her?

It is not every day that a girl gets kidnapped, starts developing feelings for her kidnapper, has him give her a brain-scrambling orgasm, gets rescued, and catches the eye of another sexy guy. All in the span of what? Thirty-six hours?

What a mess.

She smiled and gave his hand a little squeeze. "Congratulations, you must be very excited."

His answer surprised her. "I'm not sure I'm going to do it."

She halted. "Why the hell not? If I may ask?"

"Syssi is fourteen years my junior, and she barely got through it. I would rather live out the meager years I still have than die attempting immortality. Not unless I have one hell of a good reason to take such a risk." He looked at her pointedly.

Oh, boy, twist the knife, why don't you.

He couldn't have been more obvious if he'd spelled it out and submitted it in writing. So now she was responsible for him attempting or not attempting the change. Great.

What to do. What to do.

When in doubt, play it dumb.

"There is no rush. You can take your time and think it through. And if a compelling reason were to present itself, you could always change your mind. One never knows. The Fates are fickle."

Sadistic bitches is a better description... I'm sorry... please don't punish me... Amanda looked up, squinting, afraid of the bolt of lightning they might hurl her way.

"You sound like Syssi. Only when she says stuff like that, she scares the crap out of me. Her predictions always come true—one way or the other."

Thank you, sweet Fates. Andrew shifted away from dropping his boulder-sized hints to talking about his sister.

"When I tested her precognition ability and found how amazing she was, I suspected right away she might be a Dormant. That is the real story behind my research. I'm searching for people with special abilities in the hopes that some might be Dormants. Until now, I've only found Syssi and one other guy."

"Yes, I know, Michael. He transitioned at the same time as Syssi."

"I knew it! I was right!" Amanda couldn't help herself and did a little victory dance.

"Shush…" Andrew rolled his eyes toward the two mortals behind them.

"I can't help it. I'm so excited," she whispered. "I can't wait to get back to work and start searching for more Dormants. You have no idea what that means to us."

"I think I do. Good luck."

"Thanks."

The good news brought a new spring to Amanda's step. Forgotten were the little rocks poking at the soles of her feet, the look of disgust in Kian's eyes, and the whole mess with Dalhu. She felt invincible as she hurried to get to the helicopter as fast as she could without breaking a leg.

After all, if she had single-handedly found the solution to her people's greatest problem, how hard could it be to unravel the tangled knot of this mess?

Piece of cake.

CHAPTER 31: DALHU

*P*lodding between the two Guardians with his hands cuffed behind his back, Dalhu contemplated his options—or lack thereof.

Running would achieve nothing except some serious damage from the big redhead's fists or a knife between his shoulder blades from the blond. Probably both.

Though in the mood he was in, he would have welcomed the pain.

Anything to override the horrible sense of loss, of failure—something to fill the empty hole in his chest.

Unfortunately, that required energy he couldn't muster in his current state. Maybe if he just goaded them, they would beat him up for mouthing off.

He wondered if that would work.

Nah. The brother, maybe, but not these guys.
Guardians were not known to be hotheaded—too
disciplined.

Was the brother a Guardian? It seemed he was
in charge of this operation, which would suggest
he was, and he was a strong motherfucker—well
trained. But Amanda only mentioned the female
Guardian; she said nothing about having a brother
on the force.

Dalhu suspected he was missing some puzzle
pieces.

And what was the story with the mortals they
had brought with them? Since when did the
Guardian Force employ humans? Was it some new
strategy? A way to boost their measly ranks? And
how the hell had the Guardians found him
anyway?

Where had he gone wrong?

He had been so careful, thinking of every little
detail, covering his tracks so meticulously...

It doesn't matter.

It is all over.

Amanda might have prevented his field execution, but she would not be able to keep her brother
from locking him in a small dark cell and throwing
away the key.

Which would be worse than death.

Even entombment was better than that. Though it took a long time, consciousness eventually faded at some point—not so with an indeterminate prison sentence.

Maybe he could goad the fucker to attack him. Call his sister some nasty names... that would certainly do it...

But Dalhu knew he wouldn't.

As it was, by allowing a Doomer to touch her and then making it worse by defending him, Amanda had already lost her brother's respect. There was no way he was making it even more difficult for her.

His only other option was to plead with the fucker to kill him...

Like hell.

No way would he give the arrogant, condescending, pretentious cocksucker the satisfaction.

Fuck him.

Dalhu was made of stronger stuff than that.

And brother or not, no one was looking down his nose at Amanda. No one.

He would challenge the fucker to a fight for making his own sister feel like crap.

There was nothing to justify such a sanctimonious attitude.

She hadn't stolen anything, hadn't harmed anyone or herself, and as the sole owner of her own body, she was free to do with it as she pleased —without prejudice or judgment.

That brother of hers was such a hypocrite. Where were his clan's lofty ideas of freedom and equality? Of a woman's right to choose whomever she pleased?

Supposedly, this whole ancient feud between their people was the result of the mother of their clan exercising that exact right, and choosing one male over another.

Amanda's brother was no better, in attitude if not in deeds, than the scum in Dalhu's part of the world who murdered their own daughters and sisters for putting a blemish on their family's honor.

The supposed *blemish*, more often than not, was the product of being a victim of rape.

It was ironic, really, that Dalhu, a Doomer, was going to teach that supposedly progressive jerk a thing or two about the respect he ought to show his sister.

Straightening his shoulders, Dalhu lifted his head and took a quick glance behind him, but Amanda and the mortals had fallen behind. He could dimly hear the murmur of their voices, but he couldn't see her.

CHAPTER 32: KIAN

*B*arreling downhill, Kian waited till he walked off some of his anger before pulling out his sat phone to call his mother.

"We've got Amanda. Unharmed... perfectly fine, actually." Kian did his best to sound civil, hoping his mother wouldn't notice the bite he struggled to keep out of his tone.

"I told you she was fine. Never doubt me, Kian."

"I'm glad you were proven right. Is Syssi with you?"

"She is here by my side, waiting impatiently to talk to you."

"Could you put her on?"

"Here you go, sweetie," he heard his mother say as she handed the phone to Syssi.

"Oh, God, I'm so relieved. Is everybody okay? Did anyone get hurt?"

"Andrew's plan worked without a hitch, or rather despite a hitch or two…"

"Why? What happened?"

"Nothing I'm in the mood to discuss over the phone. I'll tell you when we get home."

There was a moment of silence. "You don't sound as happy as I thought you would be…" Syssi hesitated before whispering, "Did you kill the Doomer? Is that why you sound so strange?"

"No, I didn't. Though, not because I didn't want to or am such a forgiving kind of guy," he grated. "Amanda didn't let me. She practically pulled out chunks of my hair to stop me from—" *tearing his throat out.*

Oh, hell, he had almost blurted that out. Let her assume he only meant to put the fucker to sleep, permanently, with an overdose of venom… "Yeah, I probably have a few bald spots on my head."

"Oh, wow…"

"Yeah, wow is right. And that is not even the half of it. But I'll tell you the rest later."

"I guess Amanda is not next to you. Is she close by? I want to talk to her, see how she is coping, offer my support… She must be traumatized by the ordeal."

His sweet Syssi. She was on to him and was trying, very delicately, to bring him around to see things from a different perspective.

He sighed. "No, she is not. I had to get out of there and left Anandur and Brundar to deal with her and that thing."

"I hope that by 'to deal with' you don't mean 'to take care of' like in the gangster movies…"

He chuckled. "No, we are bringing the perp to the keep and rewarding him for kidnapping Amanda with indefinite free room and board in a small cell down in the basement."

"That's good… I can't wait for you guys to get home." Syssi paused and sighed. "Be nice to Amanda, Kian. She has been through enough."

He wanted to tell Syssi he would try, but that would have been a lie. Right now he couldn't even bring himself to look at his sister, let alone be nice to her. The best he might be able to pull off was to ignore her. And he wasn't sure he could do even that.

How the hell could she? Let that animal touch her? A cold-blooded murderer?

It might not have been this particular Doomer's fangs that had killed Mark, but he was part of the team that had done it. And even if that wasn't the case, he was a Doomer, for fuck's sake. A filthy, disgusting, evil creature.

"I need to speak with my mother. Could you pass her the phone?"

There was a silent pause before Syssi answered. "Yeah, sure."

She probably expected him to say he couldn't wait to hold her in his arms, or some other nice romantic thing, but he just couldn't. Not yet.

"You wish to speak with me?"

"We are bringing in the... the Doomer to be jailed in the basement. Permanently. On the remote chance that he will somehow manage to escape, or find a way to communicate with the other minions of evil, I don't want him to find out you're here. So please, don't wait for us on the roof."

"As you wish. I will await my daughter in her quarters."

Ending the call, Kian suspected that Annani humored him for now, but most likely was already planning on visiting the Doomer later on.

He could understand her desire to question the enemy, but there was no need for that. He would do the gruesome task for her, sparing her delicate sensibilities.

In fact, he was looking forward to it. And if that

made him a bad guy, so be it. He had never claimed to be a saint.

Providing an apt ambiance for his malevolent intentions, the wolf pack that had hightailed it after the explosions was back, following him from a safe distance and howling like crazy.

He wasn't worried about them attacking him, and there were enough armed men with Amanda to ensure her safety. His brisk pace had nothing to do with the pack. But it brought him to his destination well ahead of the others.

The helicopter was parked at the spot they'd agreed on, where the narrow paved road had a little shoulder, providing just enough space for the thing not to block it completely. There was no traffic this late at night high up in the mountains. But on the remote chance that some random vehicle might be passing through, the pilot had placed small flares around the chopper and had left just enough space for a car to squeeze by. A truck would be shit out of luck.

Kian climbed inside and moved to sit up front with the pilot.

"How did it go?" the guy asked.

"Mission accomplished," Kian bit out. The pilot waited for him to elaborate. "They are on their way with an additional load of two hundred and something pounds. If this thing cannot take the added weight, I have no problem with disposing of it."

It took a moment for the pilot to catch his drift, and then his face paled. "No, it's okay. This bird is designed to take ten passengers, nine in the cabin and one more next to the pilot. We changed the configuration to make more space for cargo."

Bloody civilians. He should demand that all of the Guardians learn how to fly those things; himself included. Bringing uninitiated rookies on missions was a mistake.

What if someone had been injured? Would the guy faint at the sight of blood?

Kian sighed, running his hand through his hair and wincing as he pulled on a sore spot.

Truth was, he envied the guy.

Must be nice to be so naive, to still cringe at the sight of blood, or the mere thought of carnage. It was a luxury Kian had never been afforded. Since he was scarcely more than a boy, he had witnessed and participated in enough bloodbaths to fill a lake.

It was hard to maintain humanity, or rather what mortals referred to as humanity, after seeing how little of it there was in the world and how easily it was shed. The term no longer held the same meaning for him as it did for others. He knew how little it took to incite people into becoming murderous monsters that killed, maimed and raped everyone in their path. History recounted plenty of examples, too many of which Kian had witnessed firsthand.

Being nearly two thousand years old, he had a lot of shit to carry around in his head; shit he would've gladly forgotten.

The thing was, though, history had a nasty habit of repeating itself. And if one were foolish enough to forget the lessons of the past, one couldn't recognize the pattern—the chain of events that time and again had led to catastrophes of epic proportions.

The burden of his memories, his experiences, and his deeds had hardened him, like a sharp blade, annealing him until he became a formidable weapon. He had accepted his fate and was resigned to the sacrifices he had to make, paying with bits and sometimes chunks of his so-called immortal soul until he felt hollow on the inside.

It was his fate.

But sometimes, in moments of weakness, he wished for oblivion.

Dear Fates, he prayed that if he and Syssi were ever blessed with a child, it would be a daughter.

Because, even though gender roles were changing, as a girl chances were better that she wouldn't have to go into battle and become a killer.

The act of killing tainted the soul.

It didn't matter if you killed in self-defense, or in defense of your family, or if your enemy was the lowest, evil scum that deserved to be eradicated from the face of the earth.

Once you killed another, something inside you died as well. And then it became easier and easier with each subsequent kill.

More than anything, he wished for his children to be spared that fate. And he would do his best to shield them and their mother from the ugliness of reality and his own disillusionment with humans and immortals alike.

Fucking Doomers.

It was all their fault.

Dimly, he was aware that it wasn't true. Mortals were perfectly capable of instigating wars and committing genocide without the Doomers stirring things up—as evident by the bloody history of the Maya and other primitive peoples that the Doomers had never given a fuck about.

Still, it was more gratifying to focus the blame on a particular group.

That way, he could still harbor an irrational

shard of hope that without the Doomers to poison the minds and hearts of mortals, global peace and prosperity could be achieved, and the future was not as bleak as it seemed.

But whether true or not, there was no way to get rid of the Doomers, so it was a moot point. They were too powerful, and their evil tentacles reached too far, too wide, and too deep.

Stupid girl.

How could his own sister be so fucking stupid?

And she attacked him, her own brother, to defend that scum.

If it wasn't for the "If even a little of his skin tears, I'm never going to forgive you. Ever!" she had screamed in his ear, he might have still harbored hope that she was saving the Doomer for the information that could be extracted from him, and that the whole naked thing was about her pulling a Mata Hari.

The best orgasm of her life...

As he felt the bile rise in his throat, Kian took a big gulp from his water bottle, swallowed some, then gargled and spat out the rest.

He wished he had something stronger than water with him. But in a pinch, a cigarette would work.

Pulling the pack from his back pocket, he was

surprised to see he had only two left. Evidently, the habit was back in full force.

Whatever, he had bigger problems than this insignificant addiction.

Stepping out of the chopper, he walked a few feet away and lit one of his remaining coffin nails, then took a long drag out of the thing.

Damn, it felt good.

And by the time the brothers showed up with the Doomer between them, Kian was on his second and last cigarette, and in a much calmer mood.

Which was lucky for the fucker.

"Did he give you guys any trouble?"

"Nah, he was doing the dead-man-walking thing most of the way." Anandur helped the Doomer climb inside… and buckled him in…

What the hell?

"Why are you so cordial with him?" Kian gestured with his cigarette.

"What? You wanted me to roughen him up? You should have said something…" Anandur's red brows went in tight together.

"No, I'm just surprised. Usually, you're not as… reserved."

"For one, he didn't give us any trouble, and I'm not a bully who beats up prisoners. Second, he didn't harm our girl. And if she defended him, he obviously isn't some evil abomination. And third, he doesn't stink like some of the others. Besides, he looks so dead that it would've been like kicking a corpse. Which I don't do. Not unless they stink, that is."

"I never thought I would say this to you, but you are a better man than I, Anandur." Kian slapped the guy's thick bicep.

"I'll be damned. Did you hear that, Brundar? I want you to commit this to memory for future reference and back me up when no one believes me. I actually got a compliment from the big man himself."

Kian shook his head as he stubbed out what was left of his cigarette on the heel of his boot and returned it to join the other butts in the empty box. Anandur had a knack for making him smile. The big oaf... what was it that Andrew had dubbed him? The redheaded Goliath... Nah, that was a mouthful, he'd stick with oaf... The big oaf never took anything seriously.

Nevertheless, hard as he tried, Kian couldn't dismiss the guy's assessment or fault his logic. Who would have thought that while Kian's hatred for the enemy was turning him into a psychopath, Anandur was keeping his cool? On the other hand, it wasn't Anandur's sister who the fucker had kidnapped and defiled.

"Go and knock him out. I want him unconscious until he wakes up in the dungeon."

"And who is going to carry him in? Did you see the size of that guy? Why not just blindfold him?"

"We'll manage. I don't want him to have any idea where we're taking him. Not the distance traversed, not the sounds on the way, nothing."

"Got it. A blow to the head or a tranquilizer?"

"Whichever, I don't care."

CHAPTER 33: AMANDA

*A*s they cleared the trees and the chopper came into view, Amanda's eyes immediately went searching for Dalhu.

She found him, sitting between Anandur and Brundar, his huge body slumped forward, held in place by the seatbelt he was strapped in with.

Oh, no. She felt guilt slide over her, coating her with a layer of nasty self-reproach. She shouldn't have let Dalhu out of her sight, leaving him undefended with her brother and his sidekicks. Pulling her hand out from Andrew's grip, she tore across the narrow road and leaped up into the thing.

She grabbed for Dalhu's wrist even before her knees touched the helicopter's cabin floor, searching for his pulse as she went down to kneel in front of him.

Thank heavens; he wasn't dead. But he was out like a light.

"What have you done to him?" She glowered at the brothers.

"Just a tranquilizer, the boss's orders, princess."

She eyed Anandur suspiciously. "You didn't beat him up or anything, did you?"

"And earn your wrath? No, thank you very much." Feigning offense, Anandur humphed and looked away, crossing his tree-trunk-sized arms over his chest.

"Stop bullshitting. If Kian had ordered you to do it, you would've done it in a heartbeat. My wrath, my ass... Now, move over, you two. I want to sit next to him."

Brundar got up and moved to sit in the row behind them, but Anandur ignored her, pretending to be absorbed by the view of the dark forest he was gazing at through the chopper's window.

"You too," she commanded.

"Sorry, no can do, princess. His body will soon neutralize the tranquilizer, and I'll have to dose him again. Take Brundar's seat."

"Fine." She plopped down next to Dalhu and crossed her arms over her chest.

Her feet hurt, and after a moment or two of

pouting, she bent down and took her dirty sneakers off, along with the socks. Rubbing her toes, she glanced at the back of Kian's head.

The big jerk was ignoring her. Sitting up front with the pilot, he didn't even turn around to acknowledge her presence. *Would it kill him to say something nice? Like, I'm glad you are not dead, Amanda? Or, I was so worried about you, Amanda?*

Whatever, she was too tired to deal with the supercilious prick. Syssi must have the heart of an angel to put up with that. Poor girl.

Kian didn't deserve her.

And to think she was the one who had brought those two together.

Yet instead of showing his gratitude, her brother was being an ogre.

Tears stung the back of her eyes as she imagined the very different welcome she would get from Syssi. She had no doubt her friend was waiting anxiously for her to come home and would run to hug her and kiss her and tell her how worried she'd been, and how happy she was to have Amanda back safe and sound.

Syssi was such a sweet soul... and so was Andrew...

Following after his two friends into the craft,

Andrew yanked the heavy sliding door shut, then gave her shoulder a little squeeze before heading back to join his friends in the last row.

The chopper lifted into the dark sky, barely disturbing the quiet as it kept climbing up and away.

Looking out the window, she spotted the cabin, the two upper windows still dimly illuminated by the one lamp they had left on.

For some inexplicable reason, she felt a tinge of sorrow seeing it go. And as she pondered the odd reaction, a dull ache settled in her chest.

She was going to miss it.

Heck, she missed it already.

She had been different there. Except, Amanda had a hard time putting her finger on what the difference was.

Then it hit her.

Intimacy.

It was such a foreign concept to her. Being with only one person, getting to know him, letting him see her naked.

And she wasn't referring to her body. Many had seen her unclothed. But the mask had always stayed on, her act shielding her better than any fabric ever could.

Dear Fates, sometimes she wasn't even sure

that there was something real under the façade she was projecting. After fronting the diva persona for so long, what had been initially meant as a protective layer over her fragile inner self—the self that wasn't sure, the one that doubted she could be loved and accepted for who she really was—had become her.

Whoever that was.

She was going to miss the intimacy she had with Dalhu, his unrelenting efforts to win her heart, his complete acceptance of her.

But then, there was Andrew—the sweet—with his veiled and not so veiled hints.

If it hadn't been for Dalhu, she would've responded differently to him. After all, being confirmed as Dormant, his status had changed from a potential hookup to a potential mate.

Funny, in the span of two days, she had gone from having no options to having two.

The thing was, though, once Andrew's eligibility became known to the rest of the clan's females, he would get snagged real quick.

If she had any brains at all, she would grab him while he was still single and still interested and forget all about Dalhu and their doomed relationship.

Ha. Ha. Ha.

A doomed relationship with a Doomer...
Very funny...
Not.

CHAPTER 34: ANDREW

As the chopper lifted and turned, Andrew's stomach lurched as usual upon takeoff, and he bit down the inside of his cheek to stop the rise of bile. Puking all over Amanda who was sitting right in front of him certainly wouldn't earn him favorable points.

Oh, God, the sight of her naked body. That image would forever be seared on his retinas. She was so damn perfect, she should be worshiped.

By him.

He had to have her.

Hell, he was going to.

She believed him to be such a nice guy; supportive, nonjudgmental. True, he was, though only with her... but not because he had such a cherubic disposition.

Oh, boy, had she had him pegged wrong.

Not that he was going to correct her misconception. After all, the whole point was to win her over, and he wasn't above taking advantage of her current emotional fragility. He was going to use whatever weapons were available to him.

So what if he was somewhat deceitful, or insincere? He had her best interests at heart... even if his tactics were questionable.

She would thank him later.

Her kidnapper was nothing but a lowlife scum that somehow managed to play her. And she fell for it.

Hook, line, and sinker.

Under normal circumstances, the guy could've never scored a woman like her, even if he wasn't a member of the deeply despised opposing team.

And besides, if Amanda had deluded herself into thinking Kian would allow anything between her and the Doomer, she had another think coming.

Especially after the stunt she'd pulled attacking him to defend the guy.

Her brother harbored such deeply ingrained hatred for their clan's enemies that he would never be able to see that Doomer as anything but pure evil.

Not that Andrew could fault the guy for feeling that way, or disapprove—regardless of Amanda's misguided infatuation.

There was a good reason for Kian's rabid hatred. After all, these bastards' sole mission was to kill each and every member of Kian's family and while at it drag humanity back down into the dark ages.

Amanda obviously wasn't thinking clearly, no doubt suffering from a mild case of Stockholm Syndrome. But once she'd shaken it off and come to her senses, she would run away from that Doomer straight into the arms of her only relevant alternative—the one her family would approve of. The one who'd stood by her side, offering a supportive arm, a shoulder to cry on, and a nonjudgmental ear.

Andrew smiled. The Doomer didn't stand a chance.

AMANDA & DALHU'S STORY CONTINUES IN
BOOK 4 OF THE CHILDREN OF THE GODS SERIES
DARK ENEMY CAPTIVE

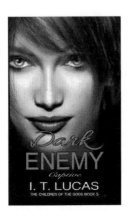

IS AVAILABLE ON AMAZON
TURN THE PAGE TO READ AN EXCERPT

Dear reader,

Thank you for joining me on the continuing adventures of the ***Children of the Gods***.

As an independent author, I rely on your support to spread the word. So if you enjoyed the story, please share your experience, and if it isn't too much trouble, I would greatly appreciate a brief review on Amazon.

Click here to leave a review

Love & happy reading,

Isabell

DARK ENEMY CAPTIVE
Book 2 in Amanda & Dalhu's Story

When the rescue team returns with Amanda and the chained Dalhu to the keep, Amanda is not as thrilled to be back as she thought she'd be. Between Kian's contempt for her and Dalhu's imprisonment, Amanda's budding relationship with Dalhu seems doomed. Things start to look up when Annani offers her help, and together with Syssi they resolve to find a way for Amanda to be with Dalhu. But will she still want him when she realizes that he is responsible for her nephew's murder? Could she? Will she take the easy way out and choose Andrew instead?

EXCERPT

*A*s the chopper began to descend, Andrew turned to the window and watched the bright helipad square on Kian's rooftop grow closer. There was a big letter A in its center that he hadn't noticed upon takeoff, and Andrew wondered what it stood for.

An A for Amanda? An A for awesome immortals? Should be an F for fucking unbelievable...

The moment the craft touched down, Syssi rushed out from the cover of the vestibule onto the open rooftop—a gust of wind catching her long hair and blowing it around her head in a mad swirl. It looked like she was cold—the poor girl huddled inside her light jacket, tucking her chin and holding the collar against her cheeks.

That got her boyfriend moving fast.

With a muted curse, Kian threw the passenger's door open and jumped down. Ducking under the chopper's slowing blades, he ran out and wrapped his arms around Syssi.

It was good that the guy's wide back obscured what must've been a passionate kiss. As much as Andrew approved of Syssi's boyfriend, it didn't mean that he was okay with seeing his kid sister engaged in anything even remotely sexual.

It must have been pure hell for Kian to find Amanda as he had—spread out naked in postorgasmic bliss. Lucky for Andrew, he'd gotten on the scene a couple of minutes later, missing the main act of her and the Doomer getting it on.

It seemed to be his thing lately. He'd also been spared Syssi's almost fatal transition, learning about it only after the fact.

Thank God, she'd pulled through.

It was better that he hadn't been there. He

would've gone crazy from worry and would've attacked Kian—consequences be damned. Someone must be watching over him, shielding him from stuff he couldn't stomach.

Though before shit had gone down at the cabin, Andrew had seen enough through the Xaver imaging equipment. He'd gotten more than an eyeful while scanning the cabin's interior. Thank God for the electromagnetic radar's crappy, pixelated display.

Unfortunately, the picture hadn't been hazy enough...

Fuck, he'd better not go there if he wanted to keep his shit together.

Besides, it was none of his business. Amanda was a big girl and could do whatever she pleased with whomever she chose—even if it was a scumbag Doomer who didn't deserve to lick the crap off the bottom of her shoes.

Andrew had no claim on her—of any kind.

Not yet.

God, seeing her naked had been like an electric shock. It had scrambled his brain and had refocused it into a singular objective—making this spectacular woman his. But he would've preferred not to have shared the experience with a bunch of other guys. Thank you very much.

The immortals he could've tolerated. After all, Kian was her brother and his bodyguards were her cousins. But not Rodney and Jake, Andrew's own buddies. After the many years they had served together, the two were like brothers to him, but that didn't mean he'd been okay with them drooling over Amanda.

His only consolation was that they would remember nothing of tonight. Including Amanda's perfect, nude body. Before heading out, they had agreed to let Kian erase the whole rescue mission from their memories upon their return.

Andrew sneaked a glance at Syssi and Kian, hoping they were done with the kissing. Damn. Not only were their mouths still fused together in a heated smooch, but Kian had lifted Syssi and was trying to carry her inside.

An argument ensued, and she pushed at his chest in a futile attempt to make him put her down. After some more back and forth, it seemed a compromise had been reached. Syssi stayed outside, and Kian wrapped himself around her like a human coat. Well, not really human, close enough though.

Even when idling, the helicopter's engine was too loud to hear the particulars of their argument, but it had been easy to get the gist of it just by observing their body language. And it was obvious that Syssi had the big guy wrapped around her little finger.

Good, so Andrew wasn't the only one who was putty in her hands.

He'd learned a long time ago that his sweet kid sister's shy and demure demeanor was misleading. Syssi never backed down from what was important to her and somehow managed to bend even the toughest and the meanest to her will.

How did the saying go? The bigger they were, the harder they fell?

True, that.

Andrew smiled, glad that the lovebirds were getting along so well.

Kian was a wise man if he'd already discovered the magic of the two most important words in a guy's vocabulary—*yes, dear.*

As soon as Amanda stepped down and took a few steps away from the helicopter, Syssi discarded the sheltering arms of her boyfriend and ran to hug her friend.

Evidently, that hug was exactly what Amanda needed, and long moments passed as the women stood in each other's arms.

It pained Andrew to see Amanda's shoulders heave as she cried in Syssi's embrace. The woman had abandoned her tough act at the first sign of loving compassion.

Kian was such a self-absorbed colossal jerk. Would it have killed him to give Amanda a hug?

When the heaving finally stopped, Amanda let go and swept a finger under her teary eyes. Casting a baleful glance at Kian, Syssi wrapped her arm around Amanda's waist and together they walked inside.

Andrew had a feeling the big guy was going to sleep in the proverbial doghouse tonight. Not that he didn't deserve it for treating Amanda like shit—regardless of the extenuating circumstances.

Judging by the murderous expression on Kian's face, he was well aware of his unfavored status, and Andrew was not going to let him mess with Rodney and Jake's memories until he had a chance to calm down.

The plan was to leave them with a memory of going on an unspecified, top-secret mission they'd agreed to be hypnotized to forget. It wasn't perfect, but the guys had to have a rational explanation, or they'd think they were losing their freaking minds. As it was, it would have been hard enough to explain the missing day. Explaining the large sum of money magically showing up in their bank accounts would have been even more difficult.

But until he made sure Kian was up to the task, Andrew's buddies would keep Brundar and Anandur company and wait in the chopper for the gurney to transport the prisoner to the dungeon.

How cool was it that they had a fucking dungeon down in their basement? Just to get a gander at that, he would've volunteered to escort the prisoner himself.

But he had to keep an eye on Kian while the guy did his thing with Jake and Rodney's memories, which might end up even more fascinating than the dungeon.

The basement could wait for some other time.

"Stay here. They may need your help," he told his friends on his way out, then headed toward Kian.

Rooted to the same spot where Syssi had left him, Kian looked like the statue of *The Thinker*—except for the sitting part.

Poor jerk.

"How are you doing, big guy?" Andrew took a furtive glance at Kian's face, checking for fangs and glowing eyes. But it seemed Kian was holding it together, as evidenced by the absence of what Andrew had learned were the telling signs of an immortal male ready for battle—or losing his cool.

"Not one of my better days, that's for sure.

Though I feel like a complete ass for saying that. I should feel relieved, grateful…" Frustrated, Kian raked a hand through his hair.

"You need sleep, buddy. You're exhausted. Everything that seems bleak now will look better after a good night's rest. Trust me." Andrew gave Kian's shoulder a light squeeze. "Are you in any shape to take care of my guys' memories? Or should they crash somewhere around here for tonight, and you'll do it tomorrow?"

"No, I'm fine. The sooner it's done, the better."

"Where do you want to do it?"

"I promised them I'd take them home and erase today's events before they fell asleep. To minimize the damage to their brains it's best to do it as soon as possible, and falling asleep right after will make it even better for them."

"I'm sure they'll understand if we change it a bit; make it easier for you."

"I'm not in the habit of breaking promises."

"You are in no shape to go driving around town after not sleeping for how long? Two whole days? Or is it three?"

"I appreciate your concern, but it is going to go down exactly as I've promised them."

"Okay, but on one condition—I'm driving."

"You got yourself a deal."

Once again, Kian surprised him. As stubborn and as obnoxious as he was, the guy wasn't above admitting weaknesses or accepting help.

A few minutes later, the gurney arrived, accompanied by a pretty petite redhead.

"Andrew, this is Bridget, our in-house physician," Kian introduced her, "Bridget, this is Andrew, Syssi's brother."

Andrew offered his hand and she took it, placing her tiny palm in his large one and giving it a short though surprisingly strong squeeze. "Welcome to our world, Andrew." The wide smile spreading across her face was as welcoming as her words. "We'll be seeing a lot of each other soon, I hope."

At first, Andrew assumed that she was coming on to him and reflexively straightened his shoulders and pulled in his abs. But then it occurred to him that it was highly unlikely. There was nothing flirtatious or coy in her demeanor.

Oh, right, she was referring to the transition.

Bummer.

"We'll see. I'm not sure about it, yet."

"No rush, take your time." She gave him a little pat on the arm and turned to go check on the prisoner.

The doctor had to wait a couple of moments as

Jake and Rodney helped the brothers transport the unconscious guy out of the helicopter's cabin and onto the gurney.

She checked his vitals before letting the brothers wheel him away, then ambled up to Andrew.

Damn, he might have gotten it right the first time.

Bridget didn't bother to conceal the up and down look over she gave him. "Come and see me before you make up your mind. I'll give you a thorough checkup to assess your general health. You'll want to know where you stand, health-wise, before deciding one way or the other."

"Sure will. Thank you."

This time, there was no doubt left in Andrew's mind that the pretty doctor wanted to get to know him better, and not strictly as a patient.

Hell, why not?

If things did not work out with Amanda, the petite redhead was an interesting alternative. Bridget was not bad at all. Quite fetching, indeed.

Andrew smirked. Either one was a definite step up from his usual. Not that he had been in the habit of dating bimbos, but a professor? A medical doctor?

He would've never considered even approaching one—out of his league.

True.

But hey, this was before discovering he was a rare specimen, coveted by beautiful immortal females.

And as it turned out, he had a thing for doctors.

———

Dalhu woke up in a dark, dingy prison cell, or so he thought. But as he raised his arm to check the time on his watch, a harsh, blinding light flooded the place.

What the hell? Bloody motion detectors?

After a couple of seconds, his pupils adjusted to the bright illumination, and he swept a quick look around, taking stock of his surroundings. The windowless room was tiny, about seven feet wide by ten feet long, and bare—save for the mattress under him. At the back, a utilitarian bathroom area extended the space by another five feet or so and was separated from the main room by a low privacy wall made of semitransparent glass blocks.

Pretty standard for a single occupancy jail cell. Except for the door, which was a monster. The thing was at least twelve inches thick, and he knew this because there was a little glass door at the bottom of it and then another one about a foot away.

So he was in solitary confinement, and they planned to provide his meals through that contraption. Smart.

Still, he'd expected worse.

Hell, these accommodations were luxurious compared to some of the places he'd stayed in. And not as a prisoner. The room was clean, free of mildew, and the mattress didn't stink. There was a clean sheet over it, and they even provided him with a warm blanket.

Both smelled new.

Other than that, there were the requisite cameras, mounted high up on the ceiling where even he, as tall as he was, couldn't reach them.

Real clever. There was nothing he could fashion a weapon from, and no real privacy.

He was going to lose his fucking mind in no time.

The situation reminded him of a scene from a silly movie he had once seen, *Rocketman*, if Dalhu remembered correctly. As part of his training for a space mission, the would-be astronaut was locked for twenty-four hours in a container about the size of this room. Passing the time singing nonstop and enacting puppet shows with his socks, he drove his competitor in the adjoining tank insane.

Maybe Dalhu could do the same. Trouble was, he didn't know any songs, and he wasn't wearing any socks.

Great, his only entertainment option was thinking about his impending torture and execution.

Or worse, torture and indefinite imprisonment.

With a muffled sigh, Dalhu got up and went to check out the facilities. Finding a new toothbrush and a battery-operated shaver inside the niche over the sink was a pleasant surprise. There was no mirror, but then he didn't need one to use either. He brushed, shaved, and showered, then got dressed, putting on his old clothes.

When he got back to the room, the first thing he noticed was the tray of food in the compartment behind the little glass door, and he took it out. Sitting on the mattress, he placed the tray on the floor in front of him. Again, he was pleasantly surprised—the coffee was excellent and the two sandwiches were loaded with cold cuts. A decent meal.

Who knew, maybe this was the worst his rich captors could dish out. He doubted anyone had taken pity on him or had cared to treat him kindly.

Unless this was meant to be his last meal. Though, if this were indeed the case, they should've at least served him a juicy steak. And a stiff drink.

Did he dare entertain hope that it had been Amanda's doing?

Nah. He knew her better than that. She would not have bothered with food. If anything, she would've been on the other side of this door, demanding to see him.

Yeah, as if there was a chance in hell she cared for him—enough to defy her brother.

Dalhu wondered whether she would visit him, at least one last time to say goodbye, or forget all about him and let him rot in here alone.

After all, she'd never claimed to have any feelings for him. And engaging in sexual activity was as meaningless for her as it used to be for him...

With her, though, it had been nothing but. More like a life-altering experience. He'd been different with Amanda, and not just in the way he'd interacted with her, but on a more visceral level...

He felt as if he'd been reborn in that cabin, reshaped to become the man she needed him to be.

Still, it might have been all one-sided.

True, she'd defended him against her own

brother. But there was a big difference between not wanting to see him dead and wanting to be with him.

Yeah.

It was time to wake up from the dream and face his grim reality. He needed to get back to the way he'd been before. Ruthless and cold would get him through this, romantic and soft would not. After sorting out his new cache of feelings and memories, he would lock it away inside the minuscule compartment dedicated to the good he'd experienced throughout his life.

Dalhu finished the last of the coffee and returned the tray to where he had found it, then went back to sit on the mattress.

With his back slumped against the wall and his elbows crossed over his up-drawn knees, Dalhu buried his face in his arms and delved into his cache of precious memories.

For a long time, it had been the memory of his mother and sister that had kept him from losing it and surrendering to the darkness around him.

The sound of his sister's giggles, the image of his mother's indulgent, loving smile—those memories had sustained him during other bleak times, and he'd desperately clung to them for decades. But inevitably, they were doomed to fade.

Amanda had gifted him with new ones.

He had so little time with her, and there had been precious few of them. But he cherished each and every one.

Aside from what he'd experienced with Amanda, and what was left of what he'd once had with his family, there was nothing else in his life worth remembering.

Hell, he would've paid good money to forget most of the crap he'd been through.

This new cache would have to sustain him for shit knew how long. Provided, he escaped execution. But just in case he got to live, he wanted to preserve every little detail of his time with Amanda.

Thank the merciful Fates for Syssi, Amanda thought as she stood in Syssi's arms and sobbed her heart out. At least one person gave a damn about her and was happy to see her come home unharmed.

She'd really needed that hug.

Leaving Dalhu behind in the helicopter wasn't easy. But he'd been out throughout the ride, and just before landing Anandur had tranquilized him again. Fates only knew how long it would take Dalhu to shake it off.

And besides, with Kian out of the chopper, Dalhu was in no immediate danger.

Later, though? Amanda could only hope that Kian would leave Dalhu alone for tonight.

"I have a surprise for you," Syssi whispered in her ear as she wrapped her arm around Amanda's waist and walked her toward the rooftop vestibule.

"I know, Andrew told me. I'm so happy for you!" Amanda pulled Syssi into another hug. It seemed as if she just couldn't get enough of those.

With Kian being a monumental jerk and giving her the cold shoulder, Syssi, with her concern and warm welcome, was treating Amanda more like family than Amanda's own brother.

Syssi punched the button for the elevator and glanced up at her. "How did Andrew.... oh, wait, you were talking about the transition?"

"Of course, silly, what did you think I was talking about?" Curiosity banishing her sad musings, Amanda ignored the ping preceding the quiet swish of the elevator doors opening.

"You'll see." Syssi pulled her inside. "The surprise is waiting for you in your apartment."

A moment later, as the doors slid open, Syssi pulled Amanda by the hand she was still holding, not letting go until they stood in front of Amanda's penthouse door. "Go ahead, open it…"

Arching a brow, Amanda turned the handle and slowly pushed open the door. Was there a Welcome Home banner hanging from the ceiling of her living room? Some balloons? Syssi was so sweet…

And what was that familiar, soothing scent?

It can't be…

"Ninni? Oh, sweet Fates, I can't believe it…" Amanda ran into her mother's open arms. The crack in the dam holding back the tears that had started in Syssi's arms became a gaping hole, and the waterworks resumed.

Amanda didn't know how long she'd cried. Vaguely, she remembered her mother pulling her to sit on the sofa and cradling her in her arms like a baby. But none of Annani's words had registered, only the effect of her soft, soothing voice.

When the last of the hiccups stopped, there was a mountain of used tissues on the floor, and a large margarita was sitting on the coffee table next to an oval platter of assorted cheeses and fruits.

One glance at the platter and Amanda started crying again.

"What is the matter, darling? You do not like the cheese? I can have Onidu take it away and replace it with another snack." Both her mother and Syssi regarded her with twin worried expressions on their faces.

"No, I like cheese, you know I do... It's just that Dalhu"—hiccup—"prepared a meal for me"—sniffle—"with cheeses and wine and fruit"—another sniffle.

"Oh, sweetheart, that does not sound so horrible. Did that Dalhu—I assume this is the name of your kidnapper—did he do something to hurt you after that meal? Is that why you are crying?"

"Noooo..." The *no* came out in a wail. But then after a few more sniffles and a hard blow into a tissue, Amanda dried her eyes and drained the margarita in two long gulps. She'd been babied enough. It was time to stop crying and behave like a grownup.

"He didn't do anything to hurt me. In fact, he was the most giving, the most attentive, the most accommodating male I have ever met. He treated me like a real princess, like I was precious, and certainly with more affection and respect than my own brother."

"I see." Annani nodded sagely.

Amanda braced herself for the lecture that was sure to follow. The one about how she wasn't thinking clearly and needed time to rest. Blah,

blah, blah. "And don't think I'm suffering from Stockholm syndrome or some other psychological crap like that." Crossing her arms over her chest, she challenged her mother with a hard glare, then added a *humph* for emphasis.

"That is not what I was going to say. But I will not tolerate this kind of language or attitude in my presence. Uncross your arms, Amanda, you are not a toddler."

"I'm sorry. It's just that from the moment Kian saw me with Dalhu, he's been a jerk to me..." Amanda wasn't up for more rejection, especially not from her mother. It would destroy her completely. But she wasn't sure how Annani would react to the news flash that her daughter had let a Doomer have sex with her. Not that they'd actually gotten that far. But Amanda wasn't going to pull a Clinton and claim oral sex didn't count.

"I think you should start from the beginning and tell us everything that happened. Unless you are tired and prefer to do it tomorrow." Annani took her hand and covered it with her other palm. "You are my daughter, Amanda, and I love you no matter what. There is nothing you can say that will change how I feel. Do not be afraid to share your burden with me. This is what mothers are for." She leaned up and kissed Amanda's cheek.

"You promise not to get mad?"

"I promise. But you look exhausted, and it can really wait for tomorrow."

"I'm beat, but I won't be able to sleep until I know… until I'm sure that you're not going to hate me for what I've done." Amanda sniffled and dropped her head onto her hands.

"Come, child, no need to be so dramatic. You can tell me everything."

DARK ENEMY CAPTIVE
IS AVAILABLE ON AMAZON
CLICK HERE FOR THE BOOK'S AMAZON PAGE

TRY THE SERIES ON
AUDIBLE
2 FREE audiobooks with your new Audible subscription!

FOR EXCLUSIVE PEEKS

JOIN THE CHILDREN OF THE GODS VIP CLUB
AND GAIN ACCESS TO THE VIP PORTAL AT
ITLUCAS.COM
CLICK HERE TO JOIN

INCLUDED IN YOUR FREE MEMBERSHIP:

- **FREE** NARRATION OF GODDESS'S CHOICE —BOOK 1 IN THE CHILDREN OF THE GODS ORIGINS SERIES.
- PREVIEW CHAPTERS.
- AND OTHER EXCLUSIVE CONTENT OFFERED ONLY TO MY VIPS.